WILD
MAGIC

CAT WEATHERILL

WILD MAGIC

Walker & Company
New York

First published in the United Kingdom in 2007 by Puffin Books,
a division of the Penguin Group
Published in the United States of America in 2008 by
Walker Publishing Company, Inc.
Visit Walker & Company's Web site at www.walkeryoungreaders.com

For information about permission to reproduce selections from this book, write to
Permissions, Walker & Company, 175 Fifth Avenue, New York, New York 10010

Library of Congress Cataloging-in-Publication Data
Weatherill, Cat.
Wild magic / Cat Weatherill.
p.   cm.
Summary: Mari and her brother, Jakob, join the other children of Hamelin as they
follow the Pied Piper into a world of wild magic, where they will remain until the
fearsome Beast identifies the child chosen to free him from a centuries-old curse.
ISBN-13: 978-0-8027-9799-5 • ISBN-10: 0-8027-9799-7
[1. Magic—Fiction. 2. Brothers and sisters—Fiction.
3. Blessing and cursing—Fiction. 4. Middle Ages—Fiction.
5. Pied Piper of Hamelin (Legendary character)—Fiction. 6. Fantasy.] I. Title.
PZ7.W35395Wil 2008   [Fic]—dc22   2008006110

Typeset by Palimpsest Book Production Limited
Printed in the U.S.A. by Quebecor World Fairfield
2   4   6   8   10   9   7   5   3   1

All papers used by Walker & Company are natural, recyclable products
made from wood grown in well-managed forests. The manufacturing processes
conform to the environmental regulations of the country of origin.

To Daniel Morden, with thanks

WILD
MAGIC

PART
ONE

CHAPTER ONE

Marianna felt fantastic. She had lost her lace cap and her dress was sticking to her back, but she didn't care. She was happy. Her head was spinning with colors. And the music—*oh!* She had never heard anything like it before. It was very simple—the same few notes played over and over again on a silver pipe—but it made her think of sunshine and meadows, and long, lazy swims in a cool, blue river.

It made her dance. It made her lift her skirts and kick her heels. Clap her hands. Smile at strangers. Spin and twirl like a leaf in the wind—and it was all because of the Piper.

The adults called him "the Ratcatcher," but not Marianna. He was far too exotic for that. She had seen endless ratcatchers—dirty little men, with faces as mean and pinched as their prey. They stalked the streets with snappy dogs or paraded through the market square, dangling dead rats from their belts.

The Piper hadn't done that. Yes, he had rid Hamelin Town of rats, but not with traps and bait.

He dared to be different. Into a sad, drab world of gray and black he had come, bunting bright in turquoise and jade. Dazzling as a dragonfly. He had played a pipe and the rats had followed, dancing till they drowned in the quick brown water of the river. They had to follow him. They couldn't resist his music. And Marianna couldn't resist it now. It was glorious. She wanted to dance. She wanted to dream. She wanted to follow the Piper.

And Marianna wasn't alone. The streets were packed with children. Every boy, every girl in Hamelin Town seemed to be there, and they were all dancing.

Except one.

A boy. Watching from the side of the road. Nine years old, a bit shabby, leaning heavily on a wooden crutch. Bent body. Thin, wasted legs. A boy not made for dancing. But his eyes were leaping, bright as buttons, not missing a thing.

"Jakob!" cried Marianna, skipping over to him. "You're not dancing!"

"I am," he said. "In here." He put his free hand over his heart. "Oh, Mari, have you ever heard anything like this before?"

Marianna shook her head. "No, I haven't. It's fabulous. I feel like dancing on the rooftops! I feel my eyes have been washed in raindrops! Everything is so bright and beautiful today. The sky is beautiful. The sun is beautiful. *You* are beautiful!" She kissed

4

her brother on the forehead and he squirmed with pleasure.

"Can you see things, Mari?" said Jakob. "Because I can. When I close my eyes, I see a wonderful land. There are open fields and shimmering rivers. Orchards full of cherry trees, pink with blossoms. The sky is full of swallows and the streams are full of salmon."

"I see a meadow," said Marianna dreamily. "It's full of ponies. Wild ponies, with long golden manes and tails. There are flowers I haven't seen before and fabulous butterflies. It's amazingly beautiful. I can't believe the Piper is taking us there! We're so lucky."

Jakob nodded. "He's taking us to Paradise, Mari. And do you know the best thing about it?"

Marianna shook her head.

"In Paradise, I'll be healed. I'll have a new body! Long legs like a baby deer and a straight back. I'll be taller, Mari! Much taller! And I won't need this." He shook his crutch. "I'll be able to run like a wolf. Faster than anyone here."

Marianna ruffled his hair. "That would be a miracle."

"It's going to happen," said Jakob. "As soon as we get there."

Marianna didn't have time to reply. A passing beggar boy had seized her hand. He pulled her close and wrapped his arm around her waist. Marianna gasped. He laughed. She laughed. They danced up the street while the adults looked on.

Great crowds of angry people were lining the streets, shouting at the Piper as he led the children through the town. Butcher and baker, tanner and tailor, fisherman, cobbler, miller, and thief—every man in Hamelin seemed to be there, straight from work. None of them had bothered washing. Marianna had never seen such an assortment of mucky faces. The women were no tidier. And what a way to behave! They were pulling their children out of the passing parade. Shaking them. Slapping them. Screaming into bewildered faces.

Why? thought Marianna. *They're doing nothing wrong. They're not stealing—they're dancing! Why can't their parents be happy for them? Why don't they dance too?*

The beggar boy swung Marianna round and round. She was starting to feel tired. Her legs would ache tomorrow! But she didn't want to stop. She wanted to follow the Piper—through the streets, out of the town, and on to Paradise. Who *didn't* want follow the Piper? Sunlight was leaping through the air to touch him. He was golden, glorious, irresistible.

Marianna had one more twirl with the beggar boy, then pulled away.

"I have a cramp," she said. "I just need a minute."

"I don't!" laughed the boy. He bowed and danced on.

Marianna stepped out of the stream of dancers and leaned back against a wall, waiting until the pain went away. Oh, here was trouble! The mayor, red faced and round, was forcing his way into the throng of children. And there was his son, Karl, dancing with the best of them. The mayor had a leather strap. He was waving it like a whip. Karl's backside would be black and blue if his father caught him. The mayor had a terrible temper.

But Karl was off, bounding down the street like a March hare. His father would never catch him. The mayor wasn't built for running. His legs were too short and his belly too big.

Marianna gazed at the hot, excited faces coming toward her. She recognized one of the dancers. It was Johann, the butcher's boy. *Oh*, she thought wearily. *I hope he doesn't want to dance with me too!*

Then Marianna saw someone behind Johann. A woman: wild-eyed, breathless, snorting like a donkey. She grabbed Johann around the middle.

Johann wriggled free and turned around. "Mother! Dance with me!"

He took hold of the woman and started to spin her. Marianna laughed. Johann's mother was a tiny thing and he was throwing her around like a pile of washing.

"No!" she gasped. She seized Johann by the elbows and forced him to stand still. "Johann! What are you doing?"

"Dancing," he replied, as if he were answering the silliest question he had ever been asked.

"Listen to me!" cried his mother. "This is a spell. An enchantment. You're not thinking right. You must stop this!"

Johann kissed her on the cheek. She shook him like a rag doll.

"Forget the Piper," she pleaded. "Remember the rats, Johann. He took them to the river, remember? He drowned them, Johann. *Drowned* them in the river. Johann, he's taking *you* to the river! You mustn't go with him. *You mustn't go with him!* Don't listen to his music, Johann. He's evil."

Johann said nothing; he simply started to laugh. In despair, the woman turned away and appealed to Marianna.

"Please!" she said. "Marianna, tell him! You're a clever girl. He'll listen to you. Tell him the Piper's evil."

"No," said Marianna, "I won't. Because it's not true. The Piper's not evil. He's the best thing that has ever happened to this town. I have never, *ever* felt this good. Never, in the whole of my life. You're old. You don't understand. We want to dance. We *will* dance! You can't stop us."

With that, Marianna took Johann by the hand and together they disappeared into the crowd of dancing children.

"No-o-o-o-o!" wailed the woman, but it was too late.

They had gone.

CHAPTER
TWO

Jakob hobbled after the other children, wondering where Marianna was. He stopped every few minutes, raised himself up on his crutch and looked for a head of bouncing copper curls, but he never found them.

The Piper was leading the children along East Street, heading for the East Gate. Jakob looked at the desperate faces as he passed by. *Everyone* seemed to be watching the parade, not just parents. Jakob spotted the miller—florid and floury, shouting the loudest as usual. He didn't even *have* children, so why was he protesting? It was none of his business, though that had never stopped him in the past. There was the mayor with a whole gaggle of councilors—and monks from the abbey. That was a surprise! Usually they distanced themselves from the affairs of the town. But there they were, their round faces pale as moonshine. And there was Steneken, the beggar man who always sat outside the Market Church, and, behind him, a group of fishwives from down by the river. Yes, everyone was there!

Except the one that mattered. Jakob scanned the faces on both sides of the road but he couldn't see his father. Where was he? It was midday. Surely he wouldn't be in the tavern this early? Jakob shook his head despairingly. *Perhaps it's better if he* is *there*, he thought. *If he were here, he'd be scolding me. Though I don't know why. I'm sure he'd be glad to see the back of me—and Marianna.*

Where *was* Marianna? Jakob tried to look over the heads of the dancers. There was some kind of commotion up ahead. The procession had reached the East Gate and still seemed to be moving forward. But the air was shrill with screams. Wild, frantic, terrified screams, as if the town were tumbling into hell and taking the townsfolk with it.

Then Jakob saw what was causing the panic. It was a bubble. A huge silvery sphere, lying right in the middle of the road, blocking the open gateway. The Piper was leading the children into it. But adults couldn't enter. Women were throwing themselves against it only to bounce right off again. Men were slashing at it with knives and meat hooks, but it was making no difference. The bubble wouldn't burst or slit. It seemed as tough as cowhide.

"There's another one blocking the West Gate!" shouted a man in the crowd. "I've just seen it. We're trapped like rats!"

Hearing this, the crowd went crazy. Parents hauled their children out of the line and tried to drag them away. But the children couldn't be held. Their hands and clothes seemed slippery. No one could get a good grip. The children wriggled free and returned to the dance.

Jakob reached the gate. The bubble billowed before him: strange, bright, silver-white. Shimmering like a pearl. He reached out and touched it. It felt incredibly soft, like a cobweb. He smiled and stepped inside. Instantly the noise of the crowd was gone. Jakob felt he had entered another world. A magical land of silence and iridescent light. Then he emerged on the far side and heard the crowd again. A spiky sound, ragged and jagged like broken glass.

But that was behind him. Before him lay the road to Paradise and that was all that mattered. Though Jakob had to admit he was a little disappointed. He thought the bubble would lead to a magnificent golden road—not the dusty, potholed track that ran east of Hamelin Town. He closed his eyes to remind himself where he was going. Oh yes! Paradise was still there and it looked better than ever. Fields full of buttercups. A waterfall with a deep pool beneath. A forest with emerald trees and soft-treading deer.

Jakob grinned and opened his eyes. He wasn't sorry to be leaving Hamelin. Marianna was somewhere up ahead, so he had no one there but his father—and he wasn't worth staying for.

He pushed on, suddenly regretting the minute he had spent daydreaming. When he was at the gate, he had been surrounded by lots of children, but now he was a straggler. And where *was* Marianna? Why wasn't she looking after him, like she usually did?

She must be with her friends, he thought. *She's so excited, she's forgotten all about me. Never mind! I'll soon catch up with her.*

But would he? The Piper was setting such a quick pace only the strongest children could stay with him. The others were strung out in a ragtag line with the youngest and weakest at the end. Jakob was there, sandwiched between a tired five-year-old and a girl who had risen from a sickbed. But after half an hour, even they were nosing ahead.

"I'll keep up," he told himself. "I will." He gritted his teeth and struggled on. Thought of the new body the Piper was promising him. He couldn't be left behind. He *couldn't*. Not this time. He had far too much to lose.

CHAPTER
THREE

Marianna paused and wiped the sweat from her brow. *Whew!* This was hard work! Walking uphill on a hot day, with nothing to drink and no time allowed for resting. She turned to see how far they had come. Quite a way! Out of town and along the eastern road . . . Now they were halfway up Hamelin Hill. In the distance, she could see the road they had taken. There was no one on it. Was the bubble still working? Good! She didn't want anyone spoiling a day like this.

She shielded her eyes from the sun and looked for Jakob. There he was! Right at the end of the line. A little bit behind the others, but not too far. She wondered whether she should go back to help him. That was her job. Her father never helped him, useless oaf that he was. No, it was always Marianna who made sure Jakob had a coat on his back and food in his belly. He relied on her for everything and she knew he would be looking for her now. Wondering where she was.

But what could she do if she went back for him? She couldn't make him walk any faster. And did she really want to leave the Piper? No! She wanted to be *nearer* to him. She hadn't seen him close-up and he looked *so* handsome. Oh, Jakob would manage! He was a strong little soldier. He wouldn't be left behind.

And the climb wasn't *too* difficult. The hill wasn't overly steep, there was a path, and the Piper seemed to know where he was going. In fact, he seemed to be there.

He was standing beside a stunted hawthorn. Above him, the hill rose sharply into a solid wall of stone. He was still playing his pipe.

But Marianna noticed the tune had changed. It wasn't a dance melody now. It was something softer, sweeter. Hearing it, she dreamed of peaches and pears and jugs of cream. They seemed so real, she could almost taste them in her mouth: a perfect taste of summer.

And something magical was happening. She could see a brilliant blue light coming from inside Hamelin Hill. It was cutting through the stone like a knife through cheese, making a door. And as she watched, the door swung open and the Piper walked through.

The children started to follow, Marianna among them. But when she reached the door she wavered. It looked dark and cold inside the hill. Could that really be Paradise? Where was the sunshine, the meadow, the ponies?

And where was Jakob? She turned to look for him, but a scruffy lad knocked into her.

"Move!" said the lad angrily. "You're blocking the way!" He forcibly turned her around and pushed her through the doorway, whether she wanted to go or not. The remaining children crowded in behind her. Marianna couldn't move. She was aware of the door closing behind her.

Jakob! Where was Jakob?

Frantic now, she forced her way back through the enchanted children. The door had nearly closed. Just a sliver of light remained: a slice of summer sunshine. But she could see Jakob outside. He was desperately struggling to reach her. His legs were buckling under him. His body was falling one way, his crutch the other. And with a look of utter despair on his face, he smashed into the ground and lay there, crumpled as a dishcloth.

"Jakob!" cried Marianna. "JAKOB!" But he couldn't hear her.

The door had closed.

CHAPTER
FOUR

Black. Thick, inky black. Marianna held her hand up in front of her face but she couldn't see it. And it was cold. So cold. When the door closed, summer had been left outside. In here it was winter. Marianna felt a cold breeze brushing across her face. She could hear dripping water. The music had gone and so had any happy feeling. She tried to move forward but other children were blocking her way. They were starting to panic. Huddling together like sheep when the wolf circles.

Then she heard a sound—*sssssp*—like a sausage sizzling in a pan. Suddenly the space was filled with light. A warm, golden glow that illuminated the walls and ceiling of the tunnel they were in. Looking over the heads of the smaller children, Marianna could see the Piper. He was holding his pipe in the air. It was glowing like a torch.

The Piper turned to the children and smiled— a strange, fleeting smile that didn't quite warm his eyes.

"Come," he said.

Marianna didn't want to go anywhere. She wanted to get out, back to Jakob. But the Piper put his still-glowing pipe to his lips and instantly Jakob was forgotten, swept away in a flurry of notes that danced in the air like mayflies. And when the Piper started walking, Marianna followed without question. They all did. The Piper had smiled. There was nothing to worry about. This was an adventure! A magical journey with the most wonderful man in the world.

They walked on. The tunnel was narrow and, with so many children jostling for space, elbows were scraped against the jagged walls. There were drips from the ceiling and puddles on the path. Marianna could feel the wetness creeping up her skirt. Her petticoat was starting to slap against her legs.

"*Yuck!*" said Karl, the mayor's son. "I'm soaking wet."

He had slipped on a particularly wet patch and now his backside was soaked. But no one seemed to care.

"I'm soaking wet," he said, louder this time.

"We're all wet," said a boy beside him. "Stop making a fuss. Enjoy yourself."

Karl scowled and walked on.

Marianna felt a small hand slipping into her own. Looking down, she saw Greta, the baker's daughter. She was no more than six years old, with a face as pretty as a buttercup in June.

"Are you on your own?" Marianna asked her. "Isn't your brother with you?"

Greta shrugged. "Don't know," she said. "We were in the shop. The music came and Fred ran off. I saw him dancing in the market square. I was dancing too. It was the best fun, wasn't it, Mari?"

"Oh yes!" said Marianna with a smile. "So you think Fredrik is here somewhere?"

Greta nodded and hugged her rag doll close.

"We'll find him eventually," said Marianna, giving her hand a gentle squeeze. "Don't you worry about that. Look at these." She pointed at the tunnel ceiling.

"Icicles!" said Greta.

Marianna smiled. "That's what they look like, but they're called stalactites. You see that water, dripping from the roof? That's been dripping for hundreds of thousands of years, *drip—drip—drip* in exactly the same place. Every drip leaves a tiny bit of stuff behind. That's how they grow."

Greta paused and gazed at the delicate formations. "They're like dragon's teeth," she said at last. "Are they cold?"

"Everything is cold down here," laughed Marianna. "Come on!"

Marianna hurried on, pulling Greta behind her. She didn't want to lose sight of the Piper. He was the most handsome man she had ever seen. He was tall and slender. Graceful as a cat. He had beautiful

18

hands with long, slim fingers and the darkest, most *heavenly* hair. It reached to his waist, straight and sleek as a horse's mane. And now, in the glow of the magic pipe, Marianna could see it was flecked with gold.

Suddenly the Piper disappeared from view. The tunnel had turned sharply to the left. Marianna heard a babble of voices. Something was happening up ahead. She gripped Greta's hand and pushed on.

"Oh!"

Marianna stopped so suddenly, the boy behind walked straight into her. But neither of them complained. The view before them was astonishing. The tunnel had opened out into something infinitely bigger. Now the ceiling was higher than a Hamelin town house. The path was three times wider. A dark stream flowed alongside. The blackness was gone. This new tunnel had its own wild, fairy glow.

"Fred!" cried Greta. Suddenly she was off, running to her brother.

Marianna walked on, taking advantage of the space and the brightness to see exactly who was in the crowd. She couldn't be sure, but it looked like every child in town. Anyone she could think of seemed to be there—except Jakob. Oh, why hadn't she spoken up? The Piper hadn't noticed Jakob lagging behind. He would have waited if he had known, wouldn't he?

Marianna felt a stab of guilt, sharp as a bee sting.

She turned her attention back to the others and tried to ignore it.

Was she the oldest in the group? No. She could see big strong lads of thirteen or fourteen. Who was the youngest? There were wide-eyed four- and five-year-olds, holding on to their older brothers and sisters. But everyone was walking. No one was being carried.

Marianna wondered why the Piper didn't want toddlers. Why did he *want* anyone? What was he planning to do?

Marianna shivered and it wasn't just from the cold. But looking around, she seemed to be the only one who was getting nervous. The other children were wild with excitement. They were linking arms and pointing out strange shapes in the rock: an angel with arching wings, a snake rearing its head. Then one of the boys found a bit that looked green and slimy.

"*Eurgh!*" he said. "Miner's sneeze!"

Everyone laughed. They were all giddy with happiness. Even Greta seemed brighter. She wasn't hugging her rag doll anymore. She was showing it the stalactites.

The Piper led them on, back into a twisting, narrow tunnel, then down a slippery flight of steps. Marianna could hear running water, getting louder and louder—and soon she discovered why. They emerged into an immense cavern, as big as a

20

cathedral, with not one but *two* waterfalls cascading down from the roof.

Marianna's jaw dropped. It was breathtakingly beautiful. The most magical thing she had ever seen in all her eleven years. And just when Marianna thought life could never, ever be better, the Piper made the moment even more wonderful.

He led them *between* the waterfalls. First they had to walk along a thin ridge of rock—slipping and sliding, trying not to fall—then across a low wooden bridge that lay between the twin walls of water.

Marianna paused as she crossed the bridge. Above her rose the waterfalls: thunderous torrents of water that cascaded endlessly from on high. Right beneath her feet was a deep pool. It rumbled and churned, sending up swirling clouds of mist. They hung in the air like ghosts. Trailed their phantom fingers across Marianna's face. Soaked her clothes. Drenched her hair—but she squealed in delight. This was surely Paradise.

When the children reached the far side of the bridge, the Piper led them up another flight of steps to a rocky platform. And there, as they all gazed at the glorious cathedral cave, Greta's brother Fredrik said what everyone was thinking.

"Well! Haven't *we* got a tale to tell the folks back home!"

Suddenly the air seemed to shatter around them, as if a diamond had been dropped. The Piper was *laughing.* A strange, eerie laugh that echoed off the cavern walls and fell back down like winter rain.

"My sweet boy," said the Piper. "You won't be telling anyone *anything*. You won't be going home."

CHAPTER
FIVE

"What do you mean—we won't be going home?"

It was Marianna who had spoken. Fredrik, like the other children, was too stunned to say a word. But Marianna was quite calm. She hadn't been shocked by the Piper's words. She felt that somewhere, deep down inside, she had known all along.

"Exactly that," said the Piper. "You won't be going home."

"Now you just listen to *me*," said an angry voice. Karl, the mayor's son, was burrowing through the crowd like a bad-tempered mole. "You brought us in here—you'd better take us out!"

The Piper's eyes narrowed as he scanned Karl's face. He knew this boy. No, he knew the boy's *father*. Loud mouths ran in the family, it seemed.

"Take us out!" cried Karl again.

"Ah, but I can't, you see," said the Piper. "You remember the door that opened? It cannot be reopened for another hundred years. That means

23

nothing to me. But to you . . . Well, you will be dead by the time it opens again."

A thick silence flooded the cathedral cavern. Suddenly it felt even colder. The little ones hadn't understood what the Piper had said but they could feel that something was wrong. Some started to cry.

The older children looked at each other in horror as the truth sank in. And then came a rumble that grew louder and louder:

"You evil, scheming, devil of a man!"

And Karl threw himself at the Piper, fists curled, eyes bulging, teeth bared.

Voomf! There was a blinding flash of light—a terrible *thump*—and Karl flew through the air backward, fast as an arrow. *Doom!* He smacked into the cavern wall and slid down into a pool below, a crumpled heap of a boy.

"Dear Lord!" cried Marianna. "You've killed him!" She wanted to run to Karl. Pull him out of the icy water. Save him. But she couldn't. Her legs wouldn't move. Like everyone else, she was frozen in fear.

"I think not," said the Piper. "I have no desire to kill him. I am simply protecting myself. Come! Our journey continues." He turned his back on her, put his pipe to his lips, and started to play.

Instantly the cavern was filled with a sweet, haunting tune that made everyone think of summer.

Hot days, when the bees drone in the lane and the fish laze in the river. Warm nights under starry skies, with sausages on the bonfire and tales before bedtime. Marianna felt the enchantment wash over her. She covered her ears with her hands. She didn't want to follow the Piper—not now. She wanted to help Karl and then she wanted to go home.

But it was no use. The magical music wormed its way between her fingers. It curled into her ears and sang to her heart. Marianna could feel her eyes glazing over, like ice freezing on a pond. Her feet started to tap in time to the rhythm. She didn't want them to, but she couldn't fight the Piper. His will was too strong. She had to follow.

Marianna glanced at Karl. He was still unconscious, lying in the pool half in and half out of the water. She felt her desire to help him start slipping away. The other children were passing her by, dancing in line like a wriggly caterpillar. Suddenly Marianna feared she would be left behind. She started to panic. Her hands dropped to her sides and she heard the Piper's music ringing round the cathedral cavern. She smiled and started to dance. And when the final child passed by, she slipped onto the end of the line and Karl was forgotten, left behind like a broken toy.

CHAPTER
SIX

An hour passed, maybe more, and still the Piper led the children on. But then Marianna noticed it was becoming brighter and warmer. Lunar blue light was playing on the tunnel walls ahead. The air was softly fragrant.

And soon Marianna found herself outside, staring at a fabulous landscape. The Piper had paused. They were standing on a steep track that clung to the side of a hill.

Marianna gazed at the extraordinary world that lay before her. A majestic moon hung low in the sky, illuminating a lush, fertile land completely enclosed by mountains. Much of it was wooded, but there were settlements here and there, with lights shining like stars. It looked homey and peaceful. Nothing was stirring except for owls, which flew over the treetops on ghostly wings, hunting for prey.

"Where are we?"

Marianna felt a warm hand sliding into her own.

It was Greta again. "Are we on the other side of Hamelin Hill?"

"Yes," said Marianna, "I believe we are. But I don't think this is our world."

"No," said Greta. "This is Paradise."

Marianna smiled, then glanced at the Piper. He was staring at the full moon. And she couldn't be sure, but there seemed to be a new expression on his face. One she hadn't seen before. He looked *anxious.*

"Come," said the Piper, and Marianna heard a strange new urgency in his voice. "Come!"

He started down the path, not bothering to play his pipe, trusting that the children would follow. Wherever he was going, he was in a hurry. There was no time for dancing now.

He led the children down the steep path, faster and faster, not pausing for breath. When they reached the bottom, they followed a goat track until it joined a lane. Here the Piper stepped up the pace until they were storming along. Then he suddenly veered left, onto a path that cut across the fields, and Marianna saw what he was heading for.

There was a standing stone, set high on a mound of earth beside a rushing river. The stone was shining in the moonlight and, as they drew closer, Marianna could see it was carved with peculiar symbols. The Piper began to climb the mound, but it was steeper than it looked. He started to struggle.

Marianna was behind him. She saw him seize his leg about the thigh, as if it were troubling him. Then he cursed and turned, and she saw his face was a mask of pain. But he battled on and eventually reached the top.

Marianna followed and found the Piper more agitated than ever. He was pacing up and down. Glancing at the moon. Urging the children to be quicker. And all the while his dark eyes shimmered like fish scales.

Then there was a flash of fire-gold feathers, and a hawk cut through the shadows and landed on the Piper's shoulder. Did it whisper something in his ear? Marianna couldn't be sure, and it seemed such a silly notion. But she definitely heard the Piper speak.

"Almost there," he muttered. The hawk seemed to nod.

Finally the last child was up. There was a chorus of coughing and gasping as they tried to catch their breath. The Piper raised his hand for silence, then his musical voice rang out through the night.

"Children of Hamelin," he said. "This is a very special moment. Everything is special. The time . . . the place . . . the stone." He elegantly waved his arm; its shadow passed across the stone like a snake. "But the most special thing here is not hard and cold like this stone." He slapped his hand against the rock. "The most special thing here is a living, breathing creature. At the moment, it doesn't know

28

how special it is. But I do. And it is very, *very* special, believe me."

The Piper smiled knowingly and went on. "Did you ever wonder why the rats came to your town? I can tell you why. It had nothing to do with the weather or the size of the harvest or plain bad luck. No! Their coming was a sign. They came because they had to. They came because somebody in the town is *special*. Somebody has the most extraordinary magic power—but they don't know it. The power within them has been hidden, unbidden, waiting in the dark like a sleeping dragon. But now it is waking up. The magic is moving, stirring. The rats could feel its energy. They were feeding off it.

"And who, you ask yourselves, is this special person from Hamelin Town? Who has this unbelievable magic power?"

The Piper paused dramatically and raised an eyebrow. He shrugged. "I confess—I don't know who it is. But I *do* know that he—or she—is with us right now."

Everyone gasped. Eyes widened. Heads turned. Mouths opened.

"And," said the Piper, "we are about to discover exactly who it is."

CHAPTER
SEVEN

The Piper glanced at the moon and placed his hand flat against the Standing Stone.

"The land you see around you is called Elvendale," he said. "It is full of elvish magic, wherever you go. But there are points in the landscape where the power is especially strong. Such points are marked by stones, like this. And when *serious* magic needs to be done, elves—like myself—will choose such a place to do it. And now, what I want *you* to do is this. I want you to come forward, one at a time, and touch the Standing Stone."

"What will happen?" asked Johann, the butcher's boy.

"Nothing," said the Piper, "unless you are the One." He smiled and beckoned Johann closer. "Touch it and see."

Johann glanced at his friends. They nodded eagerly. Someone prodded him in the back, pushing him forward.

Johann swallowed his fear. Reached out his hand. Touched the stone.

Nothing happened.

"Next," said the Piper, pushing Johann aside. "Quickly now."

A girl stepped forward. Marianna knew her. She was Birgit, a street girl who begged by the abbey.

Birgit touched the stone. Nothing.

"Next," said the Piper.

Another child came forward, then another. Dozens of hands were reaching out, touching the stone. The Piper began to pace up and down again. The hawk flew from his shoulder and sat on the stone, watching the proceedings with dark eyes. Nothing was happening.

The Piper paused and looked at the children remaining. Twelve, . . . eleven, . . . ten, . . . Who was it? *Who was it?*

Marianna stood at the end of the dwindling line, feeling sick in her stomach.

"I don't know why I'm getting nervous," she muttered to herself. "I'm not the one he's looking for. There's nothing special about me."

Two were left in front of her. Marianna could feel the palms of her hands getting sticky.

One.

"It's not me," she told herself. "I'm nothing special. Am I?"

Suddenly she wasn't so sure.

"Come here."

The Piper was right beside the stone, beckoning to her. "Touch." She could hear the tension in his voice. "*Touch!*"

Marianna sidled closer. So close she could see the color of the Piper's eyes. She had wondered whether they were brown or green. Now she knew. They were violet.

"What will happen to me?" she whimpered.

"Nothing bad," said the Piper. "Touch." He was starting to sound angry.

Marianna stepped even closer. She closed her eyes. Reached out her hand. Touched the stone.

Nothing happened.

She dared to open her eyes. The Piper was staring at her oddly. He looked puzzled, confused, unsure. She started to back away. But he leaped forward, seized hold of her wrist, and forced her hand against the stone again.

Still nothing happened.

"*NO!*" The Piper threw Marianna aside and started pacing again. Now he was like a tiger in a cage— angry, trapped, despairing—snarling to himself, snapping at the situation. Then suddenly he paused and looked at the crowd of children. At the little ones, with their cherry round faces and wet mouths. At the girls, with their braids and ribbons and adoring eyes. At the boys, with their dirty shirts and scuffed boots. Rich and poor, tall and small, tired and eager.

So young. So willing. So utterly useless.

He reached into his pocket, pulled out his pipe, and began to play. A new tune—soft as velvet, heavy as plums, with burgundy notes that sang of sleep and dreams and faraway lands. Of jewels thrown upon a beach. Of love and longing and the desire to fly.

Little Greta, looking up at him, felt something moving beneath her dress. *Feathers.* Flour-white feathers. They were pushing out of her skin, ripping her gown to shreds. And now she was shrinking, molding, transforming—though there was no pain, just joy. So much joy, she thought her heart would burst. Then Greta spread her fine new wings and, as an owl, she flew up into the moonlit sky, circled the trees, and disappeared into the night.

Her brother, Fredrik, was curling in upon himself. His nose was lengthening into a snout, with a moist black nose and smart new whiskers. His eyes were shrinking into shiny black beads. His face was covering in fur. His hands and feet were elongating and growing claws. An armory of prickles was emerging from his body. Deep in his hungry hedgehog's belly, he felt a sudden longing for worms and he was off, snuffing through the undergrowth in search of supper.

Johann, the butcher's boy, felt no desire for worms. He longed to swim. He was beside the river now, gazing at the water that rushed and sparkled at his

33

feet. His eyes were shining silver in the moonlight. His skin was quickening, shimmering with scales. His legs were joining to form one strong, star-flecked tail. He was growing fins. And then, as a salmon, Johann leaped from the rock and disappeared into the river.

Birgit, the beggar girl, had always wanted to run faster. Faster than the boys who teased her. Faster than the dogs in the count's orchard. Faster than the traders who called "Thief!" as they chased her through the market. And now she could. Her legs were long and strong. Her ears were pricked and listening. Her fur was as soft as feather down. Birgit was a hare, the most magical of creatures. She bounded away into the shadows.

And Marianna? Marianna felt herself falling forward. She put her hands out to save herself, so she didn't hit the ground. Instead, she fell on all fours and stayed there. Her ears were stretching, tight as triangles. Her nose was extending into a muzzle. Her eyes were darkening, sharpening. Her hands and feet were padding into paws. She had a tail, tipped with white. Her body was covered in a rich, russet fur. Marianna was a fox: quick and cunning, hunter and hunted. She ran into the shadows at the base of the mound, then turned and sat on her haunches. Calm and curious, she looked around.

The night was full of fluttering wings and sharpening teeth, wagging tails and running feet.

The children of Hamelin flew and crawled and wriggled and swam and burrowed and leaped and climbed and ran. Shiny otters. Black-masked badgers. Tumbling squirrels. Scattering rabbits. From a stag to a spider, a mouse to a moth—one by one they were all transformed, and still the Piper played on.

Only when the last creature had disappeared did he take the pipe from his lips. Marianna the fox watched him from the shadows. She saw a strange expression on his face: a terrible blend of anger and bitter despair. Then his head fell forward and his shoulders slumped. Surely he wasn't crying?

Marianna continued to watch. Suddenly the Piper straightened himself. He raised his head and Marianna saw there were no tears. His eyes were flashing with excitement at the thought he had clearly just had.

"The other boy!" he cried jubilantly. "Back in the caves! The mayor's son! He's the One!"

And with that the Piper bounded down the mound and disappeared into the night.

CHAPTER
EIGHT

Marianna sat quietly for a minute, deciding how it felt to be a fox. She stood up, stretched, and shook herself. Tried walking. Started running. Soon she was tearing around the mound like a born vixen.

She skidded to a halt, caught her breath, and started to gather her thoughts. The first thing that struck her was how natural her new body felt. She was moving like a grown fox. She wasn't tumbling like a cub, trying to learn where to put her feet. No, she was sleek and assured and fast. Her body fitted. She felt confident inside it. She could even control the great bushy tail, which swung in the air like a rudder, helping her turn in flight. It was heavy, but it wasn't overbalancing her.

There was just *one* strange thing: she wasn't consciously thinking like a fox. She was still thinking like Marianna. She still had the same hopes and fears and desires—at least, she believed she did. She didn't feel an overwhelming urge to hunt and forage for food. Her thoughts kept returning to the

Piper. Where had he gone? Back to Karl? And why had he looked so despairing? So angry?

Marianna smiled. She had suddenly noticed that she was holding her head on one side, just like a real fox. So this was how it would work! Her conscious thoughts would remain the same, but unconsciously she would behave like a fox. Her body would do whatever was needed to survive in this strange new world.

So now her head was tilting to one side, helping her ears to locate important sounds. Her eyes were bright and wide, taking in the moonlight, helping her to see through the darkness. Her nose was identifying perfumes: night-flowering jasmine, evening primrose. Her skin was feeling a whisper of wind, despite her thick fur. Her muscles were tensed, ready to run if need be.

Marianna suddenly realized she had never been outside at night before. *Really* outside, in the wild. She had lived her entire life within the walls of Hamelin Town. So being alone, out in the countryside after dark, was a completely new experience. Yet her body seemed to know exactly what to do. That was truly amazing.

And yes, she felt scared and bewildered and desperately lost, but most of all she felt *alive*. Joyously, wildly, dangerously alive, for the first time in her life. It was a fabulous feeling.

But then she remembered Karl and the manic

37

look on the Piper's face as he disappeared into the night. He looked positively wild. Like a wolf. Hungry. Eager. The way he had bounded off! It was scary. He had looked so determined. So strong. While Karl . . . well! The last time Marianna had seen him, he was lying unconscious in a pool of water.

For the second time that day, Marianna felt a stab of guilt, right between her ribs. *Why didn't I help him?* she asked herself. *Why didn't I do more?*

Then she remembered why. The Piper had played his pipe. She had stood there, wavering, wanting to help—then the enchantment had wrapped itself around her, taking away her will to do anything but follow.

But she wasn't enchanted now. Well, she *was*. She was a fox, and clearly that was an enchantment. But she wasn't befuddled. Her thoughts were quite clear. She knew exactly what she had to do.

She had to warn Karl.

CHAPTER
NINE

Marianna put her soft nose to the ground and started sniffing: *fff-fff-fff!* She was trying to find the scent of the Piper. It was all she could think of doing. She might be able to retrace the route back to the caves, but was Karl still there? The Piper didn't seem to think so. He had taken off in a completely different direction.

Did Karl really need warning? What would the Piper do to him? Make him touch the Standing Stone? That didn't seem dangerous, though Marianna remembered she hadn't wanted to do it. It was something about the Piper's face . . . his expression had been wrong, wrong, wrong.

Marianna found the Piper's scent and followed it into dense woodland. It was a curious scent, surprisingly sweet and heavy, like the scent of lilies. But there was a faint animal smell too. A trace of musk that reminded Marianna of a dog she used to have. It was strange that Marianna should catch that scent in the Piper's trail, but it was definitely there. No doubt about it.

Marianna ran through the wood, enjoying the sensation of being a fox. She could feel the undergrowth brushing against her belly, dampening her with dew. She could hear rats scratching and moles burrowing, rabbits running and spiders spinning. She could see the full moon above the trees, hanging like a shield on the great wall of the sky. It had reached the highest point in its journey across the heavens. Now it seemed to be lingering, watching the world below.

Eurgh! A new scent hit her, so hard she felt she had been punched on the muzzle. It was a thick, rank animal smell that shot up her nostrils, slid down her throat, and brought tears to her eyes.

Aieee! Marianna had to slow down. The smell was stealing her breath and getting stronger by the second. Something was *stinking*! Whatever it was, she was nearly upon it.

Then came the sound.

A deep, painful gasp that seemed to rise up out of the belly of the earth. Animal? Human? Elven? Marianna couldn't tell, even with her perfect fox ears. It was just something *alive*, some creature up ahead. Fighting for breath. Growling. Moaning.

Marianna slowed to a crawl. She peered between the trees and crept forward, every sense alert to danger. She could see a clearing ahead, bathed in moonlight. She found a tangle of ferns, slipped inside, and peered out, trying to discover the source of the smell and the unearthly moans.

What she saw almost made her heart stop beating.

It was the Piper.

He was ripping off his clothes. Fumbling with fastenings. Kicking off his boots. Unbuckling his belt. Pulling off his jerkin. Shrugging off his shirt.

And there wasn't skin beneath.

There was fur.

Long, coarse, red fur. All over his body but especially around the neck, where it formed an immense shaggy mane.

The Piper's body didn't seem to belong to him anymore. He couldn't control it. He was being thrown this way and that. An elbow was forced up here, a knee gave way there. He was thrown to the ground and still the convulsions went on. A hundred fists seemed to be punching him from the inside. Marianna could see the flesh on his body bulge and sink as muscles formed and tightened. Then came a terrible sound, like someone crunching beetles underfoot. But it wasn't beetle cases cracking. It was bones. The Piper moaned and growled, but still the torment went on.

His face was changing now. Stretching, stretching, longer, longer. The moans became almost unbearable and Marianna couldn't help wondering why he had to suffer so. When she had turned into a fox, there was no pain, just a strange tingling sensation. But the Piper was in agony—anyone could see that—and she could smell his fear in the stench that continued to pour from his body. It was washing over her in waves and, for one terrible moment, she thought she was going to be sick. The Piper would hear her and know she was there. But what difference would that make? Why should he care about a fox in the bushes? He had better things to worry about.

Marianna swallowed hard and the feeling passed. She took a deep breath and started to feel calmer and, when she next looked, the Piper seemed calmer too. No trace of his elven form remained. He was a beast: lean about the legs like a wolf, but with a great barrel of a body like a wild forest boar. His muzzle was long and tapered, filled with fangs like a wolf's. But he had boar tusks, sharp and deadly, one on either side. His eyes were round and golden. His body ended in a fine sweeping tail and his legs, slender as they were, looked like they could outrace the wind.

All things considered, Marianna decided the creature was more wolf than boar. But then the Beast raised itself on its back legs in a way no wolf could ever do. It stood there, bent but upright, then raised its shaggy head and howled at the moon: *owwwww!* Marianna felt the fur rise on her back, running in a terrified ridge right down to her tail. She sank lower, made herself small, and hoped it wouldn't see her.

It didn't. It was busy sniffing the wind: *FFF-FFF-FFF!* And soon it found something. A scent—surprisingly close, much desired. Its great golden eyes began to shine like lanterns.

Marianna sniffed the wind too. She couldn't catch the scent, but she could guess what it was from the gleam in those golden eyes.

It was the scent of a human. A boy. Karl.

Before she realized what that meant, the Beast had disappeared into the wood, bounding between the trees with the speed of a dozen foxes. Marianna knew she couldn't catch it, let alone overtake it. She had to forget her plan and face the truth.

The Beast would hunt down Karl. There was nothing she could do to save him.

CHAPTER
TEN

Marianna sighed and rested her head on her paws. Now that the excitement was over, she suddenly felt incredibly tired. Today she had done nothing but walk and run, from midday to midnight. Her legs were aching, her feet were sore, and she was starting to feel hungry. She didn't want to think about that, but she knew she would have to eventually.

She closed her eyes. What a day it had been! And what about tomorrow? What on earth would that bring? It was too huge to think about. "I'll just have a little snooze," she told herself. "Things always seem better after a sleep."

Marianna curled herself into a tight ball, her tail wrapped around her like a muff. She felt safe and warm, despite the woodland on all sides. She felt her breathing get heavier and slower . . . Soon she was fast asleep.

Fff-fff-fff! She woke up with a start. How long had she been asleep? *Fff-fff-fff!* Her nose was twitching all on its own. *Fff-fff-fff!* She could smell damp leaves and peat and pine needles . . . and the cloying stink of the Beast. It was coming back.

Marianna felt her hackles rise. She scanned the woodland, waited and watched. Soon she heard sobbing and shouting. Karl was being dragged through the trees by the Beast. He was begging for mercy. Pleading for his life. Marianna could hear the fear in his voice, the desperation in his cries.

The Beast crashed into the clearing, walking upright with Karl slung over its shoulder like a sack of apples. Marianna shrank into the ferns. Prayed she wouldn't be noticed. Mercifully, the Beast passed her by. But she saw Karl's face: gray with fear, eyes like coal, mouth wet with pleading.

Marianna was so terrified, she couldn't think straight. Half of her wanted to run away but the other half wanted to follow the Beast. Wanted to see things through to the end, however horrible that might be.

Suddenly the wood seemed very dark, pressing in on all sides. There wasn't a sound to be heard. Not an owl, a rabbit—nothing. She couldn't even hear the Beast anymore. But she could smell it. Its stench lingered in the air like an evil spell. And even without the smell, she knew where it was taking Karl.

The Standing Stone.

CHAPTER
ELEVEN

By the time Marianna caught up with the Beast, it was bounding up the mound toward the Standing Stone. When it reached the top, it grabbed hold of Karl with its front paws and hurled him to the ground.

Ooof! Marianna heard the breath leave Karl's body. She stayed in the shadows, not daring to move, waiting to see what would happen next.

She didn't have to wait long. In a flash of fur and fang, the Beast pounced on Karl and bit him. Karl didn't scream; he hadn't seen it coming. One moment the Beast was looming over him, blotting out the moon, and the next—he was dead.

Marianna bit her tongue. Willed herself to keep quiet, when really she wanted to howl like a demon. She wanted to close her eyes but they stayed open. It was like being enchanted all over again. She couldn't tear her head away. She had to watch. She knew she would never be able to forget what she was seeing. The appalling image would burn itself onto her memory and scar her for life. But still she watched.

For one terrible moment, Marianna thought the Beast would behave like a wild, savage dog. Karl would be shaken like a rag doll, torn limb from limb, devoured. But instead it was calm, controlled. Once it had delivered the bite, it moved away from the body, sat on its haunches, and gazed up at the stars.

And suddenly Marianna couldn't help feeling she was in the presence of something magnificent. The Beast, silhouetted against the full moon, looked regal and powerful. Noble and dignified—yet strangely humble. For all its great size, it seemed small and insignificant, sitting as it was beneath the vast starry sky. Marianna felt her heart soften toward the creature—she couldn't help it—though the feeling disgusted her.

But this magical moment didn't last long. The Beast started to become agitated. It rose to its feet and began pacing, just as Marianna had seen the Piper do earlier when things were going wrong. Was the Beast waiting for something? Whatever it was, it didn't seem to be happening.

The Beast began to punch itself, hitting its chest and legs. It turned to the moon, snapped, and growled something in its bestial tongue. It ran back to Karl's body, poked and sniffed it. But still nothing happened.

And that was when something snapped inside the

Beast. It raised itself to its full height, threw back its head, and gave a howl of such anguish, Marianna thought her own heart would break, as surely as the Beast's was breaking, there on the moonlit mound, in the shadow of the Standing Stone.

The howl died away. Silence came, wrapping itself around the scene like mist. The hawk flew in, cutting through the silence like a blade. The Beast glanced at it, and Marianna saw the golden gleam in its eyes had gone. And with a shake of its great head, the Beast leaped from the mound and disappeared into the night once more.

PART
TWO

CHAPTER
TWELVE

High on Hamelin Hill was the Piper's home. It was a complex of caves, cut directly into the hillside, with a sweeping half-moon ledge outside. Beneath the ledge there was nothing—just a sheer, deadly drop. And some mornings, Finn (as the Piper was known in this world) would stand on this ledge and feel like throwing himself down, finally bringing an end to his rotten, miserable life.

Today was one of those mornings. His body ached, as it always did after the Beast had occupied it for a night. His head throbbed from the wild energy that had surged through his veins and pounded in his ears. He felt sore and stretched. Wounded and bruised, though there wasn't a mark on him. There never was. The Beast's skin was tougher than bear hide.

No, this weariness was nothing unusual. Last night had been the same as it ever was. A mad, frenzied rampage through Elvendale, hunting and chasing. Always, *always* there was hunting and chasing. Then a return to the glade and his clothes. An endless wait while the sun fiddled below the horizon, deciding whether she would show her face to the world. Another transformation, from fur to flesh—mercifully not as painful as the opposite order. And then, finally, the long walk home, stopping only to bathe in the nearest pool. That was essential—the ritual washing away of the filth and shame.

Same as ever, then, last night. Except he hadn't eaten. That *was* unusual. There had been no killing—at least, not in the usual sense. That was why he felt so ravenously hungry now.

No killing . . . Finn didn't want to think about Karl. The Beast had never killed an elf or a human before. *Never.* It was the only thing Finn was proud of in the whole sorry affair. Now even that scrap of dignity had been torn from him.

Finn turned away from the ledge and trudged into the caves. Every room was richly furnished, with furs on the floor and tapestries on the walls. There were couches and cushions, crystals and candles. Musical instruments, magic books—it was all very civilized. Certainly not the lair of a wild animal. Finn never came home while he was still in his Beast form. Some things had to remain sacred. His home was one of them.

Finn fixed himself breakfast. Nuts and berries in goat's milk. Hot boiled pheasant eggs. No meat. That belonged to the Beast. Whenever Finn returned to his elven form, he found scraps of flesh snagged between his teeth. He tasted death on his tongue: a disgusting, rusty tang of old blood.

He could taste it now. Boy blood. The mayor's son. Come to haunt him.

Finn sighed and poured himself a cup of chamomile tea. He cut a slice of honey bread and buttered it, then cut it into four dainty squares. He concentrated on the action, finding comfort in the precision. Reassured himself that the Beast was gone. Everything was as it should be.

Except it wasn't. His head was spinning with questions.

"Why?" he said. "Why did it all go wrong?"

His knife clattered to the table. He pushed his plate away. Put his head in his hands. Started to talk, though no one was listening.

"Today should be a day of celebration. The curse—gone. The Beast—gone. The pain and the shame—gone, gone, *gone*! Two hundred and fifty years . . . Have I not suffered enough? Been punished enough?"

He left the table, returned to the ledge, and gazed upon the landscape. The whole of Elvendale lay before him, green and glistening in the morning sunshine. Stray clouds cast shadows upon the land, passing over the valley like a giant's footprints, heading home to the hills of the north.

He could see wood smoke rising from a dozen

homestead chimneys. Across the valley, elves were busy with breakfast. Kitchens were filling with laughter and light, cooking and conversation. Parents, partners, children, friends . . . They were all there, gathered around their glowing hearths.

Finn wistfully turned his gaze south to the Morvern Mountains. Was his family still there? He didn't know. So much time had passed since he had seen them last. Families change.

But some things don't.

Finn felt his gaze wandering. He tried to stop it, but he couldn't. His eyes were drawn, as they always were, down the mountains to the immense green smudge below. A place of fearsome magic, untouched by time.

The Whispering Forest. The place where it all began.

CHAPTER
THIRTEEN

The Whispering Forest was a dark, wild, unknowable place. Acres and acres of trees, tall and menacing, whispering their secrets as the centuries rolled by.

Elves never entered the Whispering Forest. It was forbidden. No one could remember the reason anymore, but they still obeyed the rule. They knew they could travel the length and breadth of Elvendale. Climb any mountain, swim any river, follow any path, explore any cave. But they couldn't enter the Whispering Forest. Even if they had lost an arrow and could see it, lying among the trees, they couldn't go in to fetch it. It was lost. Gone for good. And the strange thing was, if they returned the next day, the arrow would actually be gone. Though who had taken it, they would never discover.

Whatever the reason, it didn't matter much. Elvendale had forests that were truly beautiful, full of ferns and streams and pools of warm sunlight. But the Whispering Forest could look dark and shadowy even on the brightest days. Why would anyone choose to go to such an unappealing place?

And why would anyone choose to defy an elven law? There weren't many. Elves valued freedom and the right to roam. But they were a civilized society, and civilization is based on laws and respect for them. To break a law was an act of defiance. It was like saying, *I care nothing for you and your view of the world.*

Elves weren't like that.

But Finn wasn't a pure-blooded elf. He was half human. And it was the human blood in him that made him wild and rebellious. Made him ride into the Whispering Forest when all his companions had given up the chase. At least, that's what he told himself later, when it was too late to change anything.

It had happened one bright autumn day. Finn was out hunting with his friends. His horse, Aspen, was thundering beneath him, keeping pace with the other faery mounts. Ahead ran the hounds: twenty of them, with sleek black coats, red ears, and panting tongues. They were storming across a field, pursuing a hind—a young, female red deer—when it disappeared into a small thicket of trees.

The hounds followed. Finn heard a chorus of excited yelps, then the deer emerged and ran on. Only it wasn't the same deer. It wasn't a hind anymore. It was a stag with spectacular antlers. And it wasn't red—it was white. Pure white with a silvery sheen, like ice on a frosty morning. This was no ordinary stag. This was a living, breathing vessel of magic. It raced across the field faster than thought and, in a frenzy of baying and barking, the hounds burst out of the thicket and gave chase.

"Fly, boys, fly!" shouted Perlal, the best of the riders. He was half out of the saddle with excitement, though he was in no danger of falling. He was too good a rider for that.

Finn grinned. He didn't know if Perlal was calling to the hounds or the other riders, but it didn't matter. They were all in this together: a fast, glorious pursuit of perfect beauty.

Finn leaned forward and whispered in his horse's ear. "Run, Aspen! Like the wind!" His horse *harrumphed* and obeyed. The wind whistled past Finn's ears. His eyes sparkled with speed-tears. His hair streamed out behind, longer than Aspen's tail. Had there ever been a chase like this?

The stag leaped a boundary ditch and headed down a lane: a shadowy tunnel of green, with trees arching over on both sides. There was no way out, but the stag was swifter than the hounds and knew it. On it went, faster and faster, down the lane and into a meadow.

Beyond the meadow lay the Whispering Forest.

The stag bucked insolently and vanished into its cool, shadowy embrace. The hounds followed. By the time Finn and Perlal emerged from the lane, there was nothing to see except the tails of the pack stragglers, waving between the trees.

Perlal slowed his horse and reached for his hunting horn.

"No!" cried Finn. "What are you doing?"

"Calling back the hounds," said Perlal. "It's over. We're not going in there." He put the horn to his lips and blew.

"But we're so close!" protested Finn. "The stag was tiring. The hounds nearly had him."

"I think not!" laughed Perlal. "A creature like that will run till his legs wear down. Let him go, my friend!"

Perlal sounded his horn again. The hounds started to appear, emerging from the shadows with lolling tongues and wagging tails. The other riders arrived too, laughing and joking as they relived the drama of the hunt.

But Finn didn't greet them. He was lost in thought, staring hard at the forest. He rode to the forest edge and peered into the gloom.

"Finn!" cried Perlal. "Leave it be! The hunt is over. It is time for feasting! For making merry!" He laughed loudly.

Finn turned in the saddle and scowled at him. Perlal was shocked. Finn was in a terrible temper.

He was frowning so hard, his eyebrows met in the middle. The eyes beneath them were fierce and flinty. Colder than the caves under Hamelin Hill.

"Finn," said Perlal, serious now, "come away. You know you cannot enter that forest."

Finn said nothing, simply glared at the trees.

Perlal turned to the other riders for support. Instantly, they were by his side.

"Finn!" This was Fennon, the oldest of the group. "Come away. The forest is forbidden. The Elf King himself does not ride there."

Finn swung Aspen around. "Does not—or *dares* not?"

"Does not," replied Fennon. "He obeys the elven laws of this land and you should too."

"*Pah!*" spat Finn. "How old are these laws? Times change."

"But forests don't," said Fennon darkly. "This is wild talk, Finn. We are your friends, but there's not one of us who will ride with you if you enter that forest. Act wisely, my friend."

"You delay me," said Finn. "With every word, the stag disappears deeper into the forest and I must have him. Farewell to you all."

With that, he turned Aspen and thundered into the Whispering Forest.

"Finn!" Perlal spurred his horse forward but stopped at the forest's edge. He would go no farther.

"Perlal," shouted Fennon after him, "leave him. We've lost one friend today; let's not make it two."

"Do you really think he's lost to us?" said Perlal, coming back.

"Who knows?" said Fennon. "He may return with tales of hidden treasure. Dragons. Gold. Wonders beyond our imagination."

"He may die," said Perlal.

"Perhaps," said Fennon. "But I think not." He gazed toward the forest, with its whispering trees and hidden secrets. "I think Finn will live to curse this day."

CHAPTER FOURTEEN

Finn rode deeper into the forest, searching for any sign of the fleeing stag. The forest wasn't as dark and lifeless as it had appeared from the outside. Sunlight was filtering through the canopy of leaves, dappling the trees and daubing the earth with golden puddles. Squirrels were sifting through the fallen leaves. An emerald woodpecker drummed on a log. But there was no sign of the stag.

Then a pheasant flew from the undergrowth, protesting loudly, and Finn caught a sudden flash of silver between the trees. With a smile, he gripped the reins tighter and spurred Aspen on.

Soon he saw the stag. It was bounding through the forest, effortlessly clearing every hurdle. But no matter how fast the stag ran, Aspen kept pace. Finn howled in excitement. He knew he was riding beyond reason, endangering both his own life and Aspen's. One stumble and their necks would be broken. But he didn't care. He felt wild, free, immensely powerful—and he had to have the stag. Absolutely *had* to have it.

The stag ran on, never pausing in its stride. It knew the forest so well, it didn't need to think where it was going. But suddenly there was a tree blocking the way. An immense sycamore, recently uprooted. The stag was forced to change direction. Now it was running through unfamiliar trees. It twisted and turned—but the horse was coming closer. It leaped and dived—but the horse was coming closer. It panted and strained—but the horse was coming closer.

And then, to its horror, the stag found it had run onto a precipice—a rocky outcrop. There was no escape. It couldn't leap to freedom. There was nothing but a perilous drop below.

There was a thunder of hoofbeats. The stag spun around to face the death bringer.

It was an elf. The most beautiful elf it had ever seen. Hair as dark as a crow's wing. Eyes the color of wood violets. But the eyes were cold. This elf would show no mercy. No compassion.

Finn reached for an arrow, set it into his bow, and let it fly: *ffooooooo!*

The arrow flew through the air and hit the stag. It fell to the ground, mortally wounded. But strangely, the arrow rebounded, flew back through the air, and struck Finn in the thigh. He tumbled from his horse and the two of them—hunter and hunted—lay there, united in blood.

And then, with the light fading in its eyes, the stag

turned to Finn and cursed him: "May you never be healed. May the wound in your thigh return every month, to weep for three days and three nights, ending on a full moon. And on that night, may you be transformed into a beast. And may you hunt, over and over and over again, as you have hunted me. May you be haunted by your loathsome desire to kill, driven by your savage desire for blood. May you find no peace—just endless pain and torment—for all eternity."

The stag fell back against the earth and Finn heard the death rattle in its breath.

"Wait!" he cried. "Is there no cure? Can I never be healed? I never meant for this to happen. I was lost in the excitement of the chase. My blood was hot. I didn't think."

The stag sighed, long and deep. Its eyes closed.

"Please!" said Finn. "I must know! Can I be cured?"

"No," whispered the stag. "You cannot. But there is hope. There is always hope."

"What do you mean?" said Finn. He began to drag himself across the mossy earth, desperate to hear the stag's last words. "Where is the hope?"

The stag opened its eyes one last time. "One day, perhaps, you may pass the curse to another. In the bite of the Beast."

"Who will that be?" Finn cradled the stag's head in his arms. "A stranger? A foe?"

"A human child. One who will be as you once were. Of this world, yet not of it."

"How will I know this child?" said Finn. "Will there be a sign?"

The stag shuddered in Finn's arms. There was barely a breath left.

"Will there be a sign?"

The stag gazed into Finn's eyes. Why should it say anything more? Why should it unravel the curse it had so artfully spun? Should Finn not suffer forever? No. Nothing should suffer forever.

"Please," begged Finn.

The stag struggled, painfully gathering the last of its strength. "Rats," it whispered. "A plague of rats." Then the breath left its body and it was gone. Truly gone. It simply vanished into thin air. There was nothing left to show it had ever been there at all.

Except Finn's wound. The wound was real and the blood was real. Finn lay back on the damp earth, groaning as the pain crept up his body. He felt hot, then cold. Dizzy. He closed his eyes. His face grew damp with sweat. He bit his lip, determined not to cry out, and realized he had to do something.

He tore a piece of cloth from his shirt and bound the wound as best he could. Then he called to his horse, hauled himself into the saddle, and breathed a single word: "Home."

CHAPTER
FIFTEEN

Finn awoke in his own bed, with no memory of the journey home. His wound had been dressed. His clothes had been changed. His head rested on a pile of pillows. His body was covered with a sumptuous satin throw. He could smell the scent of roses and jasmine floating in from the garden outside. Hear his sister, going about her daily tasks.

The door opened.

"Finn!" His father, arms wide in greeting. "You join us again!"

Finn pulled himself higher up on the bed. "How long—"

"Have you been sleeping? Three days. You've had quite a fever."

"No," said Finn, shaking his head vaguely. "How long . . . till the next full moon?"

His father frowned, then started to laugh. "My son!" he said. "Your brain is befuddled. This week, next week—it doesn't matter."

"It matters to me," growled Finn. He reached for

his father's arm and gripped it so hard, the older elf could feel a bruise forming. "It matters. Tell me. When?"

"Ten days? Twelve? I can't be sure," said his father in some confusion. "Why does it matter? Son? Why does it matter?"

But Finn didn't reply, simply fell back against his pillows and closed his eyes. His father was right in a way. Ten days, twelve days—it didn't matter. It was coming. That was enough.

CHAPTER
SIXTEEN

Finn started packing the very next day. He told his sister, Beren, he was moving north. She was young, giggly, full of questions.

"Why?" she asked.

"To study magic."

"Can't you do that here?"

"No."

"Is there a girl in the north?"

"No."

"Are you taking Aspen?"

"Yes."

"Are you taking Flyte?"

Finn glanced at the window. His hawk was outside on the ledge, preening his fire-gold feathers in the warm sunshine. "Yes, I'm taking him too."

"Oh."

Beren sighed so prettily, Finn couldn't help smiling. She had always adored Aspen; clearly she had dreamed of owning him too. But she must have known Finn would never leave him behind. Horse and elf were bonded for life.

As for Flyte—well! Finn couldn't imagine life without him. He had found the bird one spring morning: a damp bundle of feathers, fallen from a nest. He had raised him and trained him. Watched him grow into the most magnificent hawk he had ever seen. And then, one day, Flyte had thanked him.

Finn had been a boy at the time. He had stood there, openmouthed, while the bird talked of care and kindness. "I'm dreaming," he had told himself. "This isn't happening." But then Flyte had pecked him sharply and assured him it was real.

Finn remembered asking him, *Are you magic?* The hawk had chuckled. *No*, he said. *But you are.*

And so it began—the awakening of Finn's magic powers. As the weeks went by, he learned that his gifts went beyond those of other elves. Understanding the language of birds was just the beginning. He discovered he could breathe underwater, bring blossom to trees, summon a storm. Best of all, he could take an ordinary object and make it magic.

He started with his pipe. It was just a simple silver flute, but Finn turned it into something special. He practiced daily, teaching himself tunes. Soon he could charm any living creature with its music. And all the time, on Finn's journey of discovery, Flyte was by his side.

Was he taking Flyte? Of course he was! The hawk was already perched on the wagon, fire-gold feathers glinting in the morning sun.

"Do you know exactly where you're going?" asked Beren.

"No."

"When are you coming back?"

A pause.

"Soon."

"Yay!" Beren clapped her hands and ran to find presents. Trinkets, pictures, . . . pretty things to remind her brother of home.

CHAPTER
SEVENTEEN

A day went by. Two days. Three. Finn had packed everything he wanted. It filled the wagon—he wasn't expecting that. But the thought of never returning made him pack more and more. Things he didn't need, like the wooden sword he had played with as a boy. His father noticed but made no comment.

Four days. Five. Time was passing. Finn was delaying. Only he knew why.

The wound had healed. The skin had pulled together and the scab had fallen away. There was nothing left except a scar, silver as a snail trail. But then, one morning, Finn awoke and felt fresh blood, wet on his leg, and knew it was time to leave.

When the dreaded moment came, his family was waiting for him by the wagon. A gray mare was harnessed between the shafts, and Beren, suspecting nothing, had decorated both with flowers. As soon as Finn appeared, she dashed forward to greet him. Finn stepped back, startled. She looked so like their mother. The dark hair . . . the mischievous smile. Someday she would be a real beauty—but he wouldn't be there to see it. Beren kissed him; he closed his eyes. There could be no tears today.

Then it was his father's turn to say good-bye. The older elf took him to one side, put his hands on Finn's shoulders and said, "Son, look at me."

Finn lifted his gaze and looked into his father's eyes. And there he saw such love and concern, he longed to tell him everything. But he didn't.

"Finn," said his father, "it doesn't have to be like this. Whatever you have done, I forgive you. You don't have to leave."

"I do," said Finn.

"You don't! That's what I'm trying to say. Whatever it is, you can still live here with us."

"I can't live with myself," said Finn bleakly. He pulled away from his father and watched Beren braiding ribbons into Aspen's mane. "I can't be trusted anymore."

His father followed his gaze and suddenly felt fear twisting inside him like an eel.

"You haven't told me the whole story, have you?" he said quietly. "The forest where you picked up the wound . . . was it the Whispering Forest?"

Finn didn't reply, but his breathing deepened.

"The deer you were hunting . . . was it a magic beast? Did you . . . exchange words?"

Still Finn didn't reply. But he didn't need to. The

look on his face told his father all he wanted to know.

"Finn," he said at last, "my heart breaks to see you go, but I won't stop you. You're an adult now. You have to make your own decisions and some of them will be hard." A sob rose in his throat. He stopped. Closed his eyes. Struggled to control himself—and Finn, watching, suddenly saw the future. He saw his father aged and withered. The worry and the grief of losing his only son had worn him down, and it was entirely his fault. He had ridden into the forest alone, but both of them would suffer for it.

The vision faded.

His father sighed. "I never thought I'd say this," he said, "but I'm glad your mother didn't live to see this day. She loved you more than life itself."

Finn reeled. Why did his father have to say that? Wasn't it enough that his heart was breaking? Did his father want to rip it out of his chest too? Because that's what it felt like.

But Finn's father wasn't being deliberately cruel. He was simply lost in his own grief. "I don't want Beren to see me like this," he said, wiping his face with his fingers. "She thinks you're bound for romance and adventure, and I won't spoil it for her." He threw his arm around Finn's shoulders. "Come! We shall smile for her sake."

He led Finn back across the courtyard, pausing only to whisper a final message into his ear: "This will always be your home, Finn, and I'll always be here. Remember that."

Finn nodded. His eyes were bright with tears and he didn't trust himself to speak. He hugged his father, held him close, kissed him fleetingly on the cheek, then clambered onto the wagon.

"Blessings to you both!" he cried, raising his hand in farewell. "Father—I will send the gray mare home, as soon as I have found somewhere of my own."

"There's no hurry," replied his father, waving him away. "Keep her if you want. Aspen is very fond of her!"

With the broadest smile he could manage, Finn clicked the reins and the wagon moved off. Aspen followed behind. The hawk circled above. Ahead lay nothing but a bleak, lonely, terrifying future.

CHAPTER
EIGHTEEN

Finn drove north, not caring where he went. On the first night he slept in a barn. On the second he camped under the stars. All the while, his wound wept and the moon waxed mercilessly. And then, all too soon, it was the third night.

Full moon.

Finn turned the wagon off the lane and onto a bumpy track. It led through woodland to a glade, and there he stopped, jumped down, and unhitched the gray mare. He glanced up. The full moon was rising, climbing into the sky like a great round beetle. Finn felt hot. Feverish. The wound throbbed. Blood was seeping through the dressing, sticking his leggings to his thigh.

"Aspen," he called softly. The stallion came forward. "You must leave me now. Take Gray with you. Return in the morning when you hear my call." He stroked the stallion's ears, running them through his hands like water. "Go well, my friend."

The stallion bowed his great head and turned

away, whinnying to the gray mare as he did. Together they disappeared into the wood.

Finn sat on the grass, his back resting against a wagon wheel. He looked at the moon again. It was clear of the treetops, heading for the highest point in the heavens. He started to chew a thumbnail. The night was so quiet, he could hear his own heart. His own breathing.

With the beat of a wing, Flyte flew from the wagon to a nearby oak. He settled. Tidied a stray feather. Watched Finn with dark eyes.

"Soon?"

Finn had asked the question but the hawk didn't reply. He knew Finn was really talking to himself.

"How will it be, Flyte? Fast? Slow? Will there . . . be pain?"

Finn's breath was coming faster now. Fast and shallow. He glanced at the moon. It hadn't moved since he last looked.

In the glade, nothing stirred. No sounds disturbed the silence. No wind in the trees. No owls in flight. Nothing.

Then a rustle and—*shooo!*—Flyte launched himself into the darkness. Seconds later he was back on his branch, ripping at the dead mouse in his talons.

Finn shook his head. While he waited for the most terrifying moment of his life, his companion was thinking only of supper. But that was how animals behaved, wasn't it? They hungered, killed, and devoured. No thought. No guilt.

Soon he would understand that.

Time passed. The moon rose higher. Finn watched it and remembered the hunt. Remembered following the silver stag as it flashed between the trees like a moon through clouds.

"Why did I follow?" he asked himself for the umpteenth time. "What spirit possessed me? Perlal, Fennon, the others—they all tried to warn me. Why didn't I listen? I can think of only one reason: my human blood. My mother's blood, hot and thick in my veins. What else could it be? The others respected the law. I alone rode into that forbidden place.

"I was enchanted—I'm sure of that now. The forest worked its mysterious magic and I couldn't resist. No, that's not true. The *human* part of me couldn't resist. Instead, it spurred Aspen on.

"Oh, how I wish I could turn back time! I would follow my friends and feast in the castle. The stag would run free to this day. And I would not be burdened with such a curse."

Finn paused for breath and, as he did, he became aware of a smell. A strange, sweet smell that turned foul on the tongue. The smell of decay.

He unlaced his leggings and pulled them from under him. The wound was festering. The flesh was rotting on the bone.

"Oh!" Finn felt faint just looking. His breath

started to come in gasps. The smell was getting stronger. It seemed to be oozing from his skin. All over his body. Such a stink.

He looked at the moon. It had reached the zenith: the highest point on its journey. It would go no higher tonight.

"No," moaned Finn. "No. Not now. Not here. I never meant it to happen. Please. Anything I can do. Anything you want from me but this. Not this—*ah!*"

No more words. Finn was thrown forward onto the ground as the first pain hit him. It ripped through his body, like a hand had reached down through his mouth, gripped his guts and pulled them right out. He writhed on the forest floor. His body was itching all over. He wanted to scratch. *Had* to scratch. He looked down at his bare legs and saw the fur. It was pushing through his skin, thick and wiry. Red as rust.

Finn tried to cry out but his tongue wouldn't let him. There was nothing but a snarl, caught somewhere at the back of his throat. He shook his head, trying to shake it loose, and it came out as a growl—so unexpected, so loud, he terrified himself. Fear: that was all he knew now. Fear and pain, fighting inside him like wild dogs. His body was a battleground, elf versus Beast, and the Beast was winning.

Finn's body was pummeled and punched, stretched and snapped. Every muscle, every fiber, every bone of his body was realigned. Fats and fluids were squeezed from old spaces and oozed into new ones. Finn could see nothing but red mist; hear nothing but white noise. He was lost, trapped in a whirlwind of transformation. And the strangest thought flashed through his brain: *Don't attack me now. I cannot protect myself.* In a few minutes, he would be the most powerful creature in the land. But until then, he was no safer than a mouse.

And just when Finn thought things couldn't get any worse—they did. The mist before his eyes started to clear, his long limbs settled, he regained his balance—but he felt his consciousness slipping away. The Beast was taking control. Finn felt like he was scrabbling up an oily slope, toes and fingers clawing, desperately trying to hold on . . . but all the while he was sliding backward, down, down, down into a black pit of nothing.

No! he cried. *No!* But it was only in his head. Nothing came from his throat but a fiendish growl.

Wild with panic, he looked around, his golden eyes showing him the forest as he had never seen it before: bright, sharp, exposed. And then his great muzzle lifted itself toward the moon, his throat opened and he howled: a bone-chilling, spine-numbing bestial moan of a howl. His wet black nose drew in a huge lungful of air and filtered it for the scent it was seeking. Blood. Finn gave a final silent sob, let go, and slid down into the darkness.

CHAPTER
NINETEEN

Cold. Wet. Bright.

Finn didn't dare open his eyes. Where was he? What was he?

He summoned his other senses. He was lying on grass: he could feel it prickling his naked body. The wetness was dew. The brightness was sunshine. A blackbird was singing. Morning had come. It was over.

He opened his eyes and saw the wagon.

"No," he said, in confusion. "I wasn't dreaming. It *did* happen." He tried to sit up, but his body ached so much, he couldn't manage it. Finally, he rolled over onto his belly and pushed himself up. He looked around. There were animal tracks beside him. There was blood too, though it wasn't his own. The wound had healed. Nothing remained except the silver scar. So where had the blood come from?

He pulled himself to his feet, using the wagon as support. *Oh!* It was no dream. His legs had surely been running all night.

He scanned the glade, noted a cloud of flies, and stumbled toward it. There he found what he was looking for. A dead deer, half eaten, lay in the long grass beneath the trees. Finn could taste blood on his breath: a stale, rusty tang. He ran his tongue around his teeth. Something was caught there. He pulled it out. Deer fur.

Finn sighed and rubbed his face with tired hands. *Water.* That's what he needed. He needed to be clean. Needed to wash away the stink and the shame.

There was a stream beyond the trees. Finn scrubbed his skin and washed his hair. Cleaned the dirt and blood from under his fingernails. Picked every shred of meat from his teeth and chewed wild peppermint to sweeten his breath. Then he returned to the wagon, dressed himself in fresh clothes, pulled out his cooking pot, and set about making a civilized breakfast.

"So," he said to himself, "that's how it's going to be. Well, at least I had fair warning. And I had the sense to return here. That's good."

He picked up his torn clothes and threw them on the fire, making a mental note to strip next time, as soon as the change began. Then he remembered the horses.

"Aspen!" he called. "Gray!"

There was no reply. Finn started to panic. What if he had attacked more than the deer last night?

"ASPEN!"

An answering whinny came from between the trees. Finn felt a wave of relief wash over him and, when the horses reappeared, he actually had tears in his eyes. He was so pleased to see them unharmed.

Soon breakfast was ready. Finn sat in a pool of morning sunshine with a bowl of porridge in his hands and a mug of mint tea by his side. He watched the horses contentedly grazing on the lush grass, and Flyte preening his feathers on top of the wagon. *How perfect is this?* he thought. *If a traveler came by and saw us now, he would never guess how different things were last night! He would see only the sunshine and the peace.*

And in that moment, Finn decided he would try to be like that imaginary traveler. He would see the sunshine, not the shadows. He would forget the panic and savor the peace. And he would try not to think about his other self—the Beast that would drag him back into the darkness in one month's time.

CHAPTER TWENTY

And so Finn began a new life. After several weeks' wandering through Elvendale, he found a home: the caves set high on the side of Hamelin Hill. But he didn't stay there permanently. He journeyed far into the world of mortal men, listening for any rumor of rats. And there were plenty. With hope in his heart, he would travel to yet another rat-infested town—and every time he would be disappointed.

There would always be a simple explanation for the increase in rats. An especially good harvest. A particularly bad winter. Sometimes it was the sheer filth of the town. People were packed into tiny houses. Houses were crammed into narrow streets. Streets were squashed onto islands, hemmed in by town walls and rivers. Back lanes were narrow, sunless, and slippery, full of whatever rubbish the townsfolk had thrown out. Rotting vegetables, night soil, dead animals . . . It was rat heaven. They would feast and breed till there were so many of them there was almost a plague.

Almost a plague. But not quite.

Again and again, Finn walked through unfamiliar streets, his heart tight with disappointment because he could count the rats. If it really were a plague, he wouldn't be able to do that. There would be too many. He would trip over them in the street. Find them on his chair, in his bed, on the table, stealing from his supper bowl.

Finn would stay a single night and move on. Sometimes he would travel to another town. Sometimes he would return to Elvendale, entering through one of the ancient doors in Hamelin Hill. Aspen would always be there to greet him, though Flyte was often away, traveling through the mortal world, hunting rumors.

But wherever Finn journeyed, the Beast went with him: a memory, a shadow, a shape that waited to become solid. Every month the wound would weep. Every month the Beast would come, and blood would be spilled beneath the full moon.

Time passed. A hundred years . . . two hundred . . . two hundred and fifty . . . and still the curse held. Finn was finally giving up hope. He started to believe he would be doomed forever; he was convinced the stag had lied to him. Its promise of a special child had been nothing but a trick. A final twist in the tale.

And then, one bright summer's day, hope returned, falling from the sky on fire-gold wings.

Finn was at home, standing on the cave ledge, gazing toward the Whispering Forest and lost in the darkest of thoughts when Flyte arrived.

The hawk dropped through the cloud veil in a hunting dive—wings pinned back, eyes on target—and landed heavily on his master's shoulder.

Finn staggered backward, regained his footing, and laughed out loud. "Flyte!" he cried. "Would you bowl me over the edge? Take care, my friend, I beg you!"

The hawk shook itself and coughed. "I have seen them."

Finn was instantly alert. There was something about the bird's energy that struck him as unusual. Flyte wasn't an excitable creature. "Rats?"

The hawk nodded. "Thousands of them."

Finn felt the breath leave his body. After so long, when he'd thought all hope was gone! He tried to stay calm—but could feel himself getting excited, like a boy at a feast.

"Thousands? Where?"

"Close," said Flyte. "So close!"

Finn held up his hand. The hawk obligingly climbed onto it and Finn brought it before his face. "*Where?*"

"Hamelin!" said Flyte, dancing up and down like a parrot. "Hamelin Town!"

CHAPTER
TWENTY-ONE

Finn entered the town from the west and paused on the bridge to scan the riverbanks. They were black with rats. Hundreds of them—thousands of them—more than he could count. A plague!

Finn was still grinning as he passed through the West Gate. Into the town he went, skirting the Abbey of Saint Boniface with its solemn stones and long shadows. Up Bakehouse Lane and on to the marketplace. And wherever he went, he saw rats. Tumbling out of doorways. Clinging to window ledges. Scuttling in and out of the gable roofs, feasting on the very fabric of the houses: straw, clay, timber. Finn could hear them scritching and scratching, gnawing and clawing.

Finn cut across the marketplace and found a low wall outside the church. Perfect! He sat down and started to study the people. But he had barely started when he was interrupted.

"You here for the rats?"

Finn turned. Beside him sat a ferrety man with

bright eyes and a face that hadn't seen water for weeks.

"You're a charmer, aren't you?" said the man, pointing at the silver pipe that protruded from Finn's bag. "From the east. You're not from these parts. I can tell by your clothes. Bright as a songbird, you are! Bright as a songbird! And just look at your hair! There's not a lady in town with hair so fine!"

Finn smiled politely and returned his attention to the townsfolk. The man was right. They were a drab lot, dressed in nothing but brown and gray and buttery cream. He was wearing a turquoise jerkin and jade leggings with a bold yellow belt and a jaunty red cap. None of the men he could see had waist-length hair.

"What are you planning to do, then, Ratcatcher?" said the man. "I only ask because we've had half a dozen ratcatchers come to town already, and they've all gone away defeated. They've tried everything. Poison, traps, dogs. But nothing works. There's just too many of them, see? They're breeding like flies in the warm weather."

Finn was only half listening. A ratcatcher? Is that really what he looked like? Well, if that's what they wanted to believe, let them! It would be a good disguise. He could wander through the streets, wherever and whenever he wanted. No one would question him or challenge his unusual appearance.

With the freedom of the town, he would surely find the special child.

"You just want to make sure they pay you enough," the ferrety man went on. "That mayor of ours will try to beat you down. A meaner man never walked this earth, I swear. You make sure he pays. In gold."

Gold! Finn smiled. He had no need of that. He had a chest full of elven gold at home, for all the good it did him. No amount of money would buy an end to the curse. But taking a job would be fun. He hadn't had one before.

"So," said the man, impatiently shaking Finn's arm, "what are you planning to do?"

"Wait and see," said Finn, tapping his nose. "Patience, my friend."

"Patience? We've had enough of that! We want results! Don't we, Miller?"

The miller had been walking past, heading for the tavern and a meeting with the butcher.

"What's that you're saying?"

"I was saying we need results, Miller, getting rid of these blasted rats. This young man here is a ratcatcher. Come from the east with his pipe, see?"

"I do!" said the miller. "And I'm wondering why he's sitting there doing nothing. Come on!" He grabbed Finn by the arm and hauled him to his feet.

"My good sir!" protested Finn. "Unhand me!" He

shook himself free. There were floury fingerprints where the miller had seized him. "What's your meaning?"

"They're up there," said the miller, pointing to a window in the town hall. "The mayor, the council—the whole rotten lot of them. I've just seen them go in. So come on! The sooner you strike a deal, the sooner you can get to work. I'll have no grain left in my mill if this goes on much longer."

Suddenly Finn found himself being manhandled toward the town hall. He couldn't escape; the crowd around him was getting larger and rowdier by the minute. The news was spreading like chicken pox. *A young man . . . ever so handsome! Says he can rid the town of rats today. Aye! Today! Every last one!*

With the miller on one elbow and a market trader on the other, Finn didn't even need to walk. He was carried along while his legs dangled beneath.

And so he was taken into the town hall. The crowd pushed past the stewards—despite their loud-mouthed protests—and stormed into the council chamber, without so much as a knock, a please, or a thank-you.

"WHAT IS THE MEANING OF THIS?" roared the mayor. He was a short man, very stout, with a red face and uncommonly small eyes. Finn thought he looked like a toadstool.

"He's a ratcatcher," said the miller, "and we want you to employ him."

"Indeed?" said the mayor, bristling at the idea that anyone should tell him what to do. "And what makes him any different from all the others we have tried?"

"He says he can do it!" shouted a voice.

Finn had said nothing of the kind, but he knew he could if necessary, so he kept quiet.

"They have all claimed that," said the mayor. "Promised miracles, half of them. Anyway, let the man speak for himself."

The mayor rose from his chair. It was set high on a dais, as befitted his lofty position within the council. From here, he had a commanding view of everything that went on beneath him, and it provided ample opportunity for theatrical flourishes. The mayor gleefully saw such an opportunity now. Regally he descended the dais steps. But he stopped when he reached the last one. He wouldn't step down to the Ratcatcher's level. Oh no! This was far enough. He peered down his nose at Finn.

"So," he said. "Can you rid the town of rats?"

Finn raised his face and the mayor found himself looking into such extraordinarily beautiful eyes, he quite forgot to breathe. And when Finn said yes, the mayor believed him. Absolutely. In that moment, he would have believed anything.

"But you will have to pay me," added Finn.

"Of course!" answered the mayor. "Just name your price."

"One thousand guilders."

It was the first figure that had come into Finn's head.

"One *thousand*?" spluttered the mayor. "That's a huge amount of money."

Finn was amused to see the mayor getting so upset over something that meant nothing to him. He smiled, turned his back on the councilors, and headed for the door.

Instantly the council chamber erupted. "Pay him!" shouted the people. "Agree! He's our only hope!" There was jostling and jeering. The stewards tried to restore order but they were hopelessly outnumbered. The councilors started to fear for their safety, although many of them agreed with the price. Already the mayor was being physically attacked. An old woman was belting him with her walking stick, hard across his knees.

"WAIT!" cried the mayor as Finn reached the door. "Wait, good sir! Your price will be met. You have my word on it. Please—rid our town of rats! Then come back here and you will be paid."

Finn smiled graciously and retraced his steps. With an elegant bow, he shook the mayor's fat hand and the deal was done.

CHAPTER
TWENTY-TWO

Finn left the town hall hoping for a little peace. He was tired and hungry. He wanted to rest before he began his search.

But the crowd wasn't going to let him escape. They were all still shouting, pulling, pushing. One woman put her hand in his bag and teased out the silver pipe.

"Ratcatcher!" she cried. "Here! Play this! Charm them away!"

"What's she mean?" asked a boy in the crowd, tugging at his mother's apron.

"She wants him to play the pipe," explained his mother. "There are men in the east . . . powerful men, who can charm snakes and birds with music. He must be one of those."

"Is he magic?" said the boy.

"No!" laughed his mother. "He's just a man. Though he is a bit special, I think. And he is *ever* so handsome." She started to blush and hoped no one had noticed.

No one had. Everyone was watching Finn. He had taken the pipe from the woman, and the cries for him to play it were so deafening, he feared for his ears. He raised his hand and held the pipe to his lips. Instantly the crowd fell silent. Then he began to play.

The notes slid from his pipe like smoke. Curled in the air, faint and delicate. The townsfolk could hardly hear them.

But the rats could.

The scritching and scratching stopped. The gnawing and clawing ceased. Thousands of heads lifted. Eyes narrowed. Ears pricked. Whiskers twitched, as if they could lift the tune from the wind. And somewhere deep inside their warm bodies, a promise was planted.

A promise of food and warmth—more and more of it. Eternal sunshine, endless feasting. Mountains of bread. Caverns of cheese. Milk. Honey. Meat. Eggs.

Where?

Close, said the music. *Within reach. Come.*

The rats came. Out of the houses and the church . . . the shops, the mills, the forges . . . the town hall and the abbey . . . the gatehouses and the tall stone towers. They tumbled and leaped and fought among themselves, trying to get closer to the music and the man who made it.

The townsfolk were screaming. There wasn't room

in the streets for everyone. So many rats! They were climbing up ladies' legs and hiding in their skirts. Falling from windows onto wigs and hats. They were biting and nipping, coughing and spitting.

Finn started to walk, with the furry parade following: out of the market square, down Fisherman's Lane, and on toward the Weser River. And here the rats from the town were joined by the rats from the riverbanks, until there was such a hot, heaving mass of bodies, the townsfolk couldn't get close. Already some were breaking away from the crowd and heading for the bridge to get a better view.

Finn continued to play, holding the enchantment as he scanned the riverbank. He noticed a small wooden jetty with a rowing boat tied to it. Perfect! He walked toward it—somewhat unsteadily. The rats were so numerous it was like walking through deep black snow. He could feel their tails cracking through his thin-soled boots. There were so many bodies, he couldn't help standing on them.

Finally he reached the boat and stepped down into it. *Hmm!* A problem! He needed to untie the rope but he didn't want to stop playing. He glanced around. There was no one close enough to see what he was doing. The townsfolk hadn't reached the bridge yet.

He took the pipe from his lips, murmured something, then carried on playing. Slowly the rope began to untie itself, like a snake uncoiling in the warmth of the sun. Then the boat slipped from its mooring and started drifting toward the middle of the Weser.

Panic! Wild, frantic panic! The rats were losing the paradise they had been promised! The food, the warmth, the eternal sunshine—everything they wanted was disappearing with the Piper. The rats had to follow. Had to.

They began to throw themselves from the jetty and riverbanks. They started to swim, following the boat, the Piper, the dream. But there were so many of them. So many! There wasn't room to kick and breathe. Some started to sink. As soon as they did, others took their place. Now the sinkers couldn't come up for air even if they wanted to.

The water started to churn. The air was cut with squeals and cries. The rats were drowning and there was nothing they could do to save themselves. The music was irresistible. It couldn't be ignored. Thousands of bodies were floating in the river, but still they came: an endless stream of rats, dancing toward death.

The town was emptying. Where they had been before, there was nothing now but silence. A strange, still silence and the distant sound of a pipe, drifting on the river.

CHAPTER
TWENTY-THREE

With the town clear of rats, Finn was able to begin his search. Every day he roamed the streets and sat in the market square, looking for the special child. How would he recognize him? Finn wasn't sure. The stag had said so little. *A human child. One who is as you once were. Of this world, yet not of it.* What did that mean? He assumed it meant a boy with mixed parents—one mortal, one elf. But he could be wrong. It could be a girl. One who had magic powers but didn't know it. He was once like that. When he was young and strange things happened around him, he explained them away as fate or fortune. Perhaps that was what the stag meant.

Finn could only hope that the child would have a special aura. Everyone had an aura: a cloud of color that surrounded the body. Auras were invisible to most human eyes, but he could see them if he wished. They were wonderfully revealing. If someone was sick, it showed in the aura. So if someone was dif-ferent—gifted—surely that would show in an aura too? He hoped so. Otherwise he would have to catch the One *doing* something magical, and that was highly unlikely, since the child probably didn't know he had magic powers.

Finn's search wasn't made any easier by the townsfolk wanting to thank him all the time. He would be sitting by the Market Church, trying to watch the passersby, when someone would come to shake his hand or give him a thank-you gift. He was never rude, but it did irritate him. While he was being polite, the child could be passing unnoticed.

A week went by. Finn had studied countless auras, but still he hadn't found the One. He was starting to panic. He appeared calm, but his head was full of niggling questions. What if there isn't a special child? What if the rats were just a freak of nature? Am I wasting my time? How long should I stay?

And then, one day, the last question was answered for him.

His wound began to bleed.

CHAPTER
TWENTY-FOUR

Three days. He could stay no longer. Finn had never been the Beast outside Elvendale, and he didn't intend to start now. Wherever he had traveled over the centuries, he had always, *always* returned home at full moon. He needed the familiarity of Elvendale around him. Despite the Beast's massive strength, he would feel vulnerable in the human world. It held too many hunters.

So now there was a new urgency to the search. Finn scanned faces by day and roamed the streets by night. He knew he wasn't seeing all the children of the town. The rich were closely guarded and seldom left their houses. Some of the poor worked day and night, then slept in locked cupboards. How could he ever find them?

Flyte circled in the sky above, hoping to catch a sign as he might a rabbit. But he had no luck either and the time went by.

One day. Two. Soon it was the third day. Finn sat outside the town hall, trying to ignore the pain in his leg. The wound was firmly bandaged but it ached constantly. Walking would make it worse, he knew, so his plan was to sit there all morning.

As usual, he was studying the children, but not as thoroughly as before. Today he had neither the time nor the energy to read every aura. He would have to be selective.

Who could it be? Was it the tall lad pushing the hay cart? No. He had a coarse face and dull eyes. No intelligence there. The crying boy? Too young. The rich girl on the pony? Possibly.

She rode closer. Finn closed his eyes and struggled to conjure her aura. How difficult it was today! Instead of seconds, it needed minutes of concentration, and every one sapped his strength further. This one required such effort, he could feel sweat forming on his brow.

It was done. Finn opened his eyes and looked at the girl again. His heart sank. No. It wasn't her.

"Ratcatcher!"

A shrill woman's voice snapped Finn out of his disappointment. Beside him stood an enormous fisherwoman, with hands as red as a pair of lobsters.

"What's this I hear?" she said, poking him with a fat finger. "You haven't collected your gold! Why ever not?"

Finn shrugged. He had forgotten all about it.

"*Ooh!*" said the fisherwoman. "I wish I could be so careless of a thousand guilders! You must be a rich one, m'lord! But joking aside, Ratcatcher, you really should collect the money, whether you need it or not. Those councilors are a slippery lot. Treacherous as Weser mud. Especially the mayor. And if you let them get away with not paying, they'll try the same trick on another poor soul, and he might need it desperately."

"I'll settle with them," said Finn.

"Good man," said the fisherwoman. "Tell you what—I'll come with you. We can do it now. Come on, handsome!"

And before Finn could protest, the fisherwoman hauled him to his feet, clasped him in her arms, and squeezed him like a squid on a haddock. He was powerless to fight; he was too stunned by the overpowering smell of fish. Then one of those red lobster hands nipped him on the bottom and, for a second time, Finn found himself being bundled into the town hall.

"He's come for his money!" bawled the fisherwoman, as they burst into the council chamber. "And he wants it *now*."

"Indeed," said the mayor, his nose creasing as the woman's odor reached him. "Then he will have to *fish* for it, because we have no money to pay him." He smiled at his little joke and glared at the other councilors until they joined in.

"You see?" said the fisherwoman angrily, turning to Finn. "I knew this would happen."

Finn raised his hand to quiet her.

"What do you mean," he said to the mayor, "you have no money to pay me? We had an agreement. I would rid the town of rats; you would pay me one thousand guilders. I have kept my side of the bargain. I expect you to keep yours."

The mayor didn't reply, simply settled himself further into his deep chair. Oh, how he loved moments like this! The drama. The power. The silence. It was so quiet in the council chamber, he could hear the flies banging against the hot windows. There was a bit of fidgeting too. Clearly some of the councilors disagreed with him, but that just made it more exciting. He wouldn't change his mind.

"We won't be paying you," said the mayor grandly. "Why should we? I only agreed because I thought you couldn't do it."

Now it was Finn's turn to fall silent. He stared at the mayor, his violet eyes shining dangerously bright. He didn't need the money—but he wouldn't let the mayor get away with this. The mayor wasn't just breaking his promise, he was breaking the faery code: the unwritten agreement between humans and faeries that had existed for countless centuries. Faeries—be they elves or sprites or pixies or whatever—would help their human neighbors whenever possible, but they must always, *always* be paid for their work. It needn't be much: a bowl of milk left by the hearth at bedtime would do. But there had to be *something* given in return.

And even if the mayor didn't realize he was dealing with someone from the faery world, there was no excuse for hard-faced swindling and lying.

"This is outrageous!" cried the fisherwoman. "He did his job. He got rid of the rats, every last one."

"Exactly," sneered the mayor. "So what's he going to do now? Stand in the river and play his pipe until the rats come back from the dead?"

Finn's eyes narrowed like a cat's. He was hot. He was in pain. He was losing time, hope, and patience. He had studied a hundred auras and still hadn't found the child he wanted.

There had to be another way.

"Well?" said the mayor. "Will you? Will you charm the rats all over again?"

"No, Mayor," muttered Finn. "Not this time."

And he marched out of the town hall, put his pipe to his lips, and began to play.

PART
THREE

CHAPTER TWENTY-FIVE

Jakob struggled up Hamelin Hill, cursing his twisted legs. The Piper's music pumped through his veins. His head was filled with visions of Paradise and his heart longed to be there. But the climb was proving unbelievably hard. He was gasping for air and getting a sharp pain in his side for good measure. His crutch felt heavy and unwieldy. It was made for streets, not rough ground.

But the struggle would be worth it, wouldn't it? The Piper was taking them to Paradise. That was what he had promised. He hadn't actually *said* it, but Jakob could see it in his mind's eye: a beautiful place full of birds and butterflies, rainbows and endless sunshine. And there, in Paradise, Jakob would be healed. His legs and back would straighten. He would grow tall. He would put on weight, because there would be good things to eat, as much as he wanted. Nobody went to bed hungry in Paradise, Jakob was sure of that.

He paused to catch his breath, shaded his eyes, and

peered up the hill. It was difficult to see clearly—there was so much glare from the sun—but he could make out figures and still hear the glorious music. The worrisome thing was, everyone seemed so much farther away than before. They were leaving him behind.

"WAIT!" he yelled, as loud as he could. "PLEASE WAIT! YOU KNOW I CAN'T WALK AS FAST AS YOU!"

But they didn't wait. The Piper hadn't noticed Jakob was falling behind, his sister was nowhere to be seen, and everyone was lost in the enchantment. Their feet danced them onward, upward. Their heads were filled with their own dreams of Paradise.

Jakob started to panic. He had so much catching up to do.

He gritted his teeth, thumped the crutch into the earth, and heaved himself on. Sweat began to trickle down his face. It ran into his eyes and made him blink, but he didn't stop to wipe it away. There was no time.

He peered ahead. The group had stopped. Thank the Lord! He was getting closer now; soon he would be with them.

There was something more. A bright blue light, coming from inside Hamelin Hill, cutting through the rock, making a door. A door that was slowly opening . . .

"Nearly there," Jakob told himself. "Nearly there."

Nearly there, but not near enough.

The Piper was stepping through the door. The children were following. The door was starting to close.

"NO!" cried Jakob. He threw himself forward, every fiber in his body straining to reach it in time. One, two, three steps. Four, five, six—*aah!*

Jakob was falling. His crutch had struck a stone and toppled him sideways. Down, down, down he went—*so slowly* . . . It was unreal. It felt like time was bending. He could see the earth coming up to meet him. See his crutch falling away like a scaffolding pole. See his arms reaching out to break his fall.

He could see Paradise. A slice of Paradise, framed by the closing door. There was a tree—a cherry tree—heavy with blossom. Pink petals on the ground beneath. *Butterflies!* Sunshine. Dazzling, golden sunshine, just as he had pictured it. And there was Marianna! She was looking right at him.

But the door was closing. The gap was getting smaller and smaller.

Jakob started to crawl toward it. Rocks cut into his knees, pebbles pushed into his hands, but he didn't care. He scrabbled and fought his way toward the door, crying, "No, no, no, no, no, no, NO!"

But it was too late. The door had closed. Marianna had gone. The Piper had gone. The children of Hamelin had gone. Paradise had gone.

Jakob was alone on the hillside.

CHAPTER
TWENTY-SIX

How long did Jakob sit there? He didn't know. Time seemed to have no meaning anymore. He had lost Paradise—and Marianna. They had been snatched from him and it hurt. Hurt so badly that the cuts and bruises on his body meant nothing. The pain was deep inside, hard as a stone. The Piper had gone, but not his enchantment. That was firmly lodged in Jakob's heart. And he knew that till his dying day, he would dream of what might have been.

What was he to do now? If he returned to Hamelin, the people would demand answers. They would seize hold of him, shake him, shout in his face, "Where's my boy? My beautiful boy? My daughter? My angel? My princess?"

What could he say? Nothing would make their pain go away. And did he want to go home without Marianna? She was the one who loved him, clothed him, and managed to feed him even when the larder looked empty. Most of all, she protected him. Who would stop Papa if she wasn't there?

Jakob's father wasn't a bad man; he knew that. It was the drink that had ruined him. When Jakob's mother was alive, he rarely drank—just a flagon or two on feast days. But now he went to the tavern most nights and some mornings, and when he was drunk, he was violent. He would lash out for no reason. Pick fights with strangers. Rage and bellow in the middle of the night, waking the neighbors. Sometimes Marianna had to drag him in off the street. Usually she got shouted at for her pains, but she didn't seem to care. "Rather me than you, little brother," she would whisper as she slid back under the blankets. *Oh, Marianna!* thought Jakob. *How will I survive without you?*

It was starting to get dark. Jakob looked at the bleak, empty hillside and realized he was ravenously hungry. What could he do? Where could he go?

Home. He had to go home, whether he wanted to or not. What else could he do? He was nine years old with twisted legs and a bent back. No one would give him a job, and without a job he would starve.

With a sigh, he clambered to his feet and started the long trek home. But he was barely halfway there when he saw the people of Hamelin storming toward him. The crowd was jagged and angry, bristling with weapons. Pitchforks, spades, axes, scythes, hooks—the men had brought whatever they could find.

Clearly the Piper's magic had worn off. The people had been able to burst the bubbles and leave the town. Now they were hunting the Piper, fueled by hours of anger and frustration.

"LOOK! LOOK THERE! THERE'S ONE!"

The townsfolk broke into a run and soon the mob was upon him. Jakob was grabbed by a strong pair of hands and given a shaking.

"Where are they?"

It was the miller. A fine cloud of white flour rose from his apron as the shaking went on. "Where are they? What's the Piper done with them?"

Jakob stared at him, rabbit eyed, saying nothing.

"Are you deaf as well as lame?"

"*Oi!*" said a woman, digging the miller angrily in the shoulder. "There's no need for that. Can't you see the lad's scared?"

"Aye," said the blacksmith, shoving the miller aside. "Let him be."

The blacksmith was a great bear of a man who stood a full head and shoulders taller than anyone else. He put a comforting hand on Jakob's shoulder. "There's nothing to be scared of, lad," he said. "You've done nothing wrong. We just want to know where the others are."

Jakob wanted to help but he couldn't speak. So much had happened. He was tired and confused. Tears welled in his eyes.

"Where did they go? Jakob—where did they go?"
A soft, kind voice. Jakob turned and saw one of his neighbors.

"Into the hill," he said.

"All of them?"

"All of them. Except me."

Jakob hung his head in shame. But no one noticed. The crowd had turned into a many-headed monster that wailed and moaned and screamed and roared.

"Can you show us where?" cried the miller, spinning Jakob round.

Jakob shrugged. "There's nothing to see. The door has disappeared."

"Show us anyway," said the blacksmith, and he picked Jakob up and swung him onto his shoulders.

And so Jakob returned to Hamelin Hill, riding on the giant's shoulders. And he couldn't help thinking, *On any other night, this would be incredible.* With his head high above the ground and his legs gripped in the blacksmith's huge hands, Jakob felt like a hero, leading his army into battle. He felt strong, proud, invincible. But he knew what lay ahead and it soured things for him, even though he wanted to enjoy the ride.

The townsfolk weren't going to find the door. At first, they would be shocked and confused. Then disappointed . . . despairing . . . and finally angry.

Very, very angry. They would want to kill the Piper. And if the Piper couldn't be found, they would take their anger out on someone else.

Jakob knew exactly who that would be. Him.

CHAPTER
TWENTY-SEVEN

Jakob was right. The people of Hamelin did take their anger out on him. But that came later. First they mobbed the mayor.

It was the miller who started it, but it was the blacksmith who smashed down the mayor's front door. Jakob, watching from the back of the crowd, was astounded. Usually the blacksmith was the calm voice of reason, but not today. He swung his mighty hammer and—*CRRP!*—the doorframe buckled under the blow. The lock shattered. The door swung open.

The crowd surged in. Furniture was looted. Food was taken. The mayor and his wife were dragged out of the house, sat upon two of their own chairs, lifted high into the air, and paraded up and down the street. They were pelted with vegetables, spat upon, and sworn at. They were soaked with slop water, thrown by the bucketful from windows above. Their chairs were thumped with sticks to terrify them further. And that wasn't the end of it.

"To the river!" shouted the miller, and the crowd roared its approval.

Off they went through the streets: a great, swaying mass of people. It was as if the Piper had come to town again.

But this time, there was no drowning. The mayor and his wife thought it was going to happen. The miller *wanted* it to happen. But the blacksmith finally started to see sense and calmed everyone down. And so the mayor and his wife were simply thrown out of town, with a couple of hastily packed bags hurled after them.

Jakob was glad to see them go. He didn't approve of their rough treatment but, like everyone else, he blamed the mayor for losing the children. He missed Marianna and longed for her to return. He missed the others too, though he didn't have many friends among them.

The town was strange now. It was quiet and joyless. No one seemed to laugh anymore and no one ran in the streets. Usually there were children running everywhere: chasing balls, chasing one another, running errands, running away from trouble. But now the streets were full of orderly people, calmly going about their daily business, with no fun or mischief involved.

And there was Jakob, stumping up the street, reminding everyone of what they had lost. Heads turned, eyes narrowed, and tongues wagged wherever he went. At first, people muttered under their breath, but as time went by, they started to say things out loud so he could hear them. Cruel things that cut him to the bone. He knew they didn't mean to hurt him—they were hurting too—but it didn't make the comments easier to bear.

Jakob wanted to tell his father about his troubles, but he knew it would be a waste of time. He wouldn't show him any sympathy. His father—Simen Moller, a struggling shoemaker—should have been pleased to still have his son, but he wasn't. People had been saying things to him and he didn't like it. He felt they resented him. Envied him. Hated him even. Grief does strange things to people, he knew that. But hadn't he suffered too? Losing his wife to the fever?

Serena had been beautiful. Long, copper-colored hair cascading to her waist. Eyes that smiled whenever they saw him. A mouth like a plum, ripe with kisses.

She had been soft and gentle, kind and patient. They didn't have much money, but she never complained. If she couldn't fill their home with furniture, she said, she would fill it with love. And she did. There was always laughter and singing. And then, when the babies came, there were lullabies and stories at bedtime.

Moller would sit on the stairs while Serena settled the children. Her words would drift down to him, softer than snowflakes, but they carried such wisdom. Listening to them, he saw wonders—dragons and castles, forests and oceans—right there on the stairs in a tiny house on a back street in Hamelin.

But then the fever came to town. It stalked the streets. Prowled the alleys. Lingered in lanes. Trailed its hot fingers over innocent faces and stole the breath from anguished bodies. Whispered wetly into sleeping ears, *Come, my friend. Your time on earth is ended.*

Serena was the first to go. She tried to fight the fever, but she was like an icicle facing the heat of summer. She died as she had lived. Quietly.

Moller was consumed by grief. He saw no reason to get up in the morning, and would have lost his business if Marianna hadn't pleaded with him to carry on for all their sakes. He started to drink. Secretly at first: a bottle or two while Jakob and Marianna slept. But soon it was more and everyone suffered.

Night after night he went to the tavern. Left alone in the dark, Marianna would comfort Jakob with her mother's stories. When those were no longer enough, she invented her own. But soon—too soon—they would hear the stumble in the street and the fumble with the door latch. The stories would be over. Moller was home.

Marianna always told Jakob to stay under the blanket. She went downstairs and faced their father.

Did what had to be done to get him to bed. But sometimes Moller would just stand there, staring at her, not saying a word. Marianna never knew why he did that—but Moller did. It was because Marianna looked so like her mother. And just by being there, she reminded him of what he had lost. At moments like that, Moller found it very hard to deal with his daughter. At moments like that, he simply wanted to die.

CHAPTER
TWENTY-EIGHT

Jakob sat in the dark, thinking about Marianna. How he missed her! She had been gone for more than three weeks and life was almost unbearable without her. He didn't have a home anymore; he lived in an unkempt house with a man who was as changeable as the weather. Moller could be dark and brooding, stormy or frosty. Sometimes he was calm and almost warm. But he was never, ever sunny.

Jakob never knew what would come in through the door.

CLLLKK.

The door latch had been lifted. Now the door was swinging open. Jakob stiffened. Papa was home much earlier than expected—and he was in the wildest mood Jakob had ever seen.

Moller had been in the tavern. The miller had picked an argument with him, saying he was a lout, an idler, a boneheaded loser. Moller had tried to punch him; two men had held him back. But when the miller started on the memory of Serena, no one could hold him. And now he was home. Bruised, bloodied, and lost in a whirlwind of despair.

Jakob was terrified. His father had never, *ever* hit him, even in his bleakest moments, but now . . . Jakob had never seen Moller so upset. Tonight anything was possible.

Jakob did the only thing he could think of. He scuttled to a corner and made himself small. Covered his head with his hands and hoped he wouldn't get a beating.

But Moller had no desire to hurt his son. Yes, he wanted to hit something, but he turned to the wall for that, not Jakob. He punched until his knuckles bled. Then he fell to the floor and started to cry: huge, desperate sobs that racked his whole body. Jakob was appalled.

All that night, Jakob stayed there in the corner, wondering what he could do to make things better. And finally, just as the first fingers of dawn were creeping through the shutters, he had a brilliant thought. He would find a way into Hamelin Hill. It made perfect sense. He would find Paradise and be healed. His father wouldn't have to put up with him anymore. The townsfolk wouldn't have to look at him. He would be with Marianna. Everyone would be happy.

Could he find a way in? Jakob had no idea, but he was determined to try. He would go there that very night.

119

CHAPTER
TWENTY-NINE

Jakob left town in the early evening. By dusk he was on Hamelin Hill, searching for any sign of a door. The light was fading but that didn't matter. The Piper had been an elf, Jakob was sure of that, and elves came out after dark. That's what his mother had told him. She said they danced in the moonlight and feasted on raspberry pudding and honey cakes.

The moon started to rise. Nocturnal creatures appeared from their hiding places and began the nightly search for food. Jakob saw a badger, a weasel, and a flurry of bats—but no elves.

Jakob waited on the hillside. He waited while the moon journeyed across the sky and he was still waiting when the sun peeped sleepily over the eastern horizon. Nothing had happened. The door into Hamelin Hill had remained firmly closed.

Bitterly disappointed, Jakob started for home.

He reached his house just as his father was starting work.

"Where've you been?"

Moller was in a good mood, as he often was in the morning. Jakob found it strange, but Moller never remembered the wretchedness of the night before. Never remembered what he had said or done, no matter how awful it had been.

"To the hill."

"Why?" Moller seemed interested. Jakob was surprised.

"I was trying to get in."

"Why?"

Jakob shrugged. "I wanted to find Marianna. Paradise. The Piper."

His father smiled wryly. "Forget it, lad. You won't get in there, not if you sit on that hillside for the rest of your life. And you want to forget about Paradise. It ain't for the likes of you and me. Here—take these."

He thrust a pair of shoes under Jakob's arm.

"They're for George Wulf. West Street. Be quick now! He needs them this morning."

Jakob went back out into the street. His father's words were echoing in his head. He closed his eyes and tried to make sense of them. Eventually he sighed, opened his eyes again, and looked up. There was a strip of sky between the overhanging roofs of the houses, blue as a bird's egg. It was going to be a glorious day.

"You're right, Papa," Jakob said to himself.

"Paradise isn't for the likes of you. But it is for the likes of me, and you'll never make me think otherwise. I will sit on that hillside for *years* if I have to, until I find a way in. One night a door will open, I know it, and I'll be there when it does."

Jakob was right. One night a door *did* open and he was there to see it. And it happened much sooner than he was expecting.

CHAPTER
THIRTY

Hamelin Hill, four nights later.

Jakob shifted uncomfortably. He had been sitting on the hillside for three hours and his muscles were starting to go to sleep.

He reached into his pocket, pulled out a garlic sausage, and began to eat. He gazed at the stars and started to pick out the constellations. The Great Bear, . . . the Eagle, . . . the Swan, . . . But then, out of the corner of his eye, he saw what he had been waiting for. *The blue light!* He spun around.

It wasn't where he expected it to be. He was sitting where the Piper's door had been but this door was farther over. Twenty, maybe thirty, steps to his left. The blue light was cutting through the earth. Soon it would open.

Jakob reached for his crutch and hauled himself up. He started to cross the stony ground. Closer . . . closer . . . he was going to make it. The door began to open. *Shadows!* Two tall figures were emerging from the hill.

Jakob threw himself facedown on the ground and hoped the elves hadn't seen him. He heard a few whispered words and caught a new scent in the air. The scent of a forest. Damp earth. Pine needles.

How long before they're gone? he wondered. He decided to wait another minute.

Then he realized he didn't *have* another minute. The door would be closing and he was still some distance away. He pulled himself up in a panic, not caring if the elves saw him. He was right—the door was starting to close, slowly swinging on its silent hinges. The fan of blue light was getting slimmer and slimmer as the outside world was shut out, banished, excluded from the world within the hill.

"No!" cried Jakob. "Not this time!" He rushed forward and threw himself through the gap. *Doof!* He landed like a sack of turnips—so hard he nearly knocked his teeth out. But he didn't care. He had done it. He was inside Hamelin Hill.

He looked around. There were three carved stone arches in front of him with black tunnels beyond. But he didn't have time to study them. He turned to see the great door closing behind him, cutting him off from the only world he knew. The last thing he saw outside was a single star, shining bright. Then it was gone. Darkness descended. Jakob was alone.

CHAPTER
THIRTY-ONE

Jakob couldn't believe anywhere could be so dark. The tunnel was completely and utterly black. He waited awhile, hoping his eyes would grow accustomed to it, but they didn't. He would have to rely on his other senses to find a way forward.

He listened carefully. Nothing. He sniffed the air. It smelled fresh rather than stale, but other than that—nothing. He would have to rely on touch.

He was sitting in a puddle, that was obvious. The whole place was damp. Bone-bitingly cold. There was a faint breeze blowing in from somewhere. *The tunnels!*

Jakob felt for his crutch, found it, and ran his fingers over its length. He had fallen so heavily, he was worried it had snapped under him. Luckily it was still in one piece.

He stood up and moved forward a few steps, then paused and stretched out his hand. He could feel one of the three stone arches, smooth beneath his fingers. His hand explored a little farther. The walls beyond were wet and rough.

Jakob suspected this was the middle arch. He shuffled to his right and found the second, then shuffled back past the middle and found the third. They all felt exactly the same.

"I don't know which one to choose," he said to himself. "I don't know if they go up or down or what." He shook his head, as if that would help him decide. It didn't. "Oh, bother!" he said at last. "Middle!"

He started down the tunnel, his crutch thudding on the rock floor. *I hope the roof stays where it is,* he thought. *If it suddenly gets lower, I'll knock my head off!*

But as it turned out, the height of the tunnel wasn't the real danger ahead. There was something much more dangerous: a steep flight of steps that descended into the bowels of Hamelin Hill.

Jakob stood no chance of seeing it.

Whoa! Down he went, tumbling over and over and over again into the inky blackness. His head was safe—he instinctively curled up as soon as he fell—but he banged his knees and bumped his elbows and bounced down the stairs like a ball—*bedoying, bedoying, bedoying!*—while his crutch clattered down beside him.

Oooof! He finally hit the bottom and lay there groaning. His eyes stayed shut, trapping him inside his own little world of pain. But when he eventually opened them, he found brightness. Something was illuminating the tunnel with a soft green light. And when Jakob looked for the source, he was amazed to find it was his crutch. It was shining with a strange phosphorescent glow. And he couldn't be sure, because the crutch was lying a fair distance away, but it looked fancier somehow. Smooth and polished.

Jakob started to crawl toward it. He could feel tender bruises on his knees, but other than that, his legs seemed fine. No, they were *more* than fine. They were working. He wasn't pulling with his arms like he usually did, drawing his legs up behind. He was crawling on all fours. His legs were bearing his weight.

Jakob stopped and sat up. Now he was kneeling, with his legs beneath him and his hands resting on his knees. He had *never* been able to kneel before.

Suddenly he felt cold all over. Was he . . . ? No, he couldn't be. And yet . . . Could he? Really . . . walk?

There was only one way to find out. Jakob leaned forward and placed his hands on the ground. Took a deep breath. Pulled one of his legs up from under him, then the other. Now he was crouching. He took another deep breath and started to raise himself up.

Up he went, to his usual height—and beyond. His back was straightening. His shoulders were leveling.

His legs were firm and strong, rooting him to the ground. He was standing tall for the first time in his life, and it felt fantastic.

Jakob looked down at his new body. His britches were too short now, but who cared about that? He could walk! He could probably run and jump too. He wanted to try, there and then, but the ceiling was too low. Later! He would do it later, once he was out of the tunnel.

Suddenly he remembered the crutch. He walked over and picked it up. He was right. It *was* smoother. All the rough edges had gone. The wood was clean and polished. And as he held the crutch in his hand, Jakob felt a strange vibration begin. A pulse, deep inside the wood. Something was moving, changing. The crutch started to stretch and lengthen. For a terrible moment, Jakob thought it was turning into a snake, but it wasn't. It was simply straightening itself, just as Jakob's legs had done. When it had finished, it was a beautiful staff, with a round wooden globe at its end. A globe that shone with a pearly green light to illuminate the way.

Jakob gazed at it, mesmerized. Just holding it in his hand, he started to feel different. Bold, strong, and proud, like a wizard in one of Marianna's tales. A spell-spinning, troll-tricking, dragon-slaying sorcerer who knew all things and feared no foe.

It was a wonderful feeling. Staff in hand, he marched boldly on down the tunnel.

CHAPTER
THIRTY-TWO

The tunnel twisted and turned, taking Jakob deeper into Hamelin Hill. He passed through cavern after cavern and each was more beautiful than the last. Stalactites hung from the ceiling, stalagmites rose from the floor, and where the two met they formed exquisite columns, smooth as skin. Sometimes the deposits fell in huge, frozen waterfalls, tinted with minerals: green, red, gold. And wherever he went, there was the sound of dripping water and the same cool breeze playing across his face.

There were other tunnels leading away from the main one, but Jakob ignored them, trusting his to be the easiest. Then, to his horror, he heard voices and saw flickering lights coming toward him. His new confidence vanished. He leaped into a side tunnel and stuffed the globe under his shirt, hoping its light hadn't been seen already.

He flattened himself back against the wall and tried not to breathe. Cursed his terrified heart for thumping so loudly. "Why am I so scared?" he asked himself. "Elves are friendly, aren't they?" Suddenly he had no desire to find out. He waited, while the voices grew louder. Two, maybe three, voices, speaking a language he didn't understand.

In a flash of green velvet, the speakers swept by. They were definitely elves: tall, handsome people, just like the Piper, with long flowing hair, bright eyes, and a stealthy, catlike grace to their movements. Luckily for Jakob, the elves were so lost in conversation, they didn't notice anything unusual. They strolled on.

Jakob waited a few seconds, then dared to breathe out. He wondered again: why was he so scared? Was it because of the dark? Usually he wasn't scared of darkness or enclosed spaces, but this was different. He felt trapped. He didn't know the way out— if indeed there *was* a way out. And there was so much soil above him. A whole hill's worth, pressing down.

He hadn't been expecting this. Where had Paradise gone? When the Piper opened the hill, he had seen it, hadn't he? A cherry tree, sunshine, and butterflies. He hadn't seen wet, dark tunnels.

Perhaps that was why he felt scared. He wasn't with the Piper. He felt like he was trespassing—going where he shouldn't go, seeing things he shouldn't see. If the Piper was with him, that would be different. He would be a guest. As it was, he felt like a spy. No wonder he was nervous.

Jakob pulled the globe out from under his shirt

and hurried on. But the tunnel seemed to go on forever. Was he walking around in circles? He didn't know. How could he tell when everything looked the same?

He could feel himself starting to panic and didn't like it. "Stop this!" he told himself. "It's not helping! Stay calm, keep walking and you'll find a way out. It won't be far."

Jakob was right to be optimistic. Just five minutes later, he came to an immensely long flight of steps and, as he climbed, he noticed the atmosphere was changing. The air grew sweet with the scent of roses and honeysuckle. The bone-chilling cold became a soft, welcoming warmth.

The steps led to yet another tunnel—but Jakob could see light at the end of it. Sunshine.

He started to run. His feet pounded the ground. His arms pumped the air. And just for that moment, he forgot where he was and lost himself in the joy of running. He threw back his head, laughed out loud, and ran into the sunlight. Jumped up and down and tried to touch the sun. And it was only when he collapsed onto the ground, panting but happy, that he remembered where he was.

Jakob looked at the landscape around him. He was high on the side of a hill, gazing down upon a lush valley. He could see a river, blue as a swallow's wing, with herds of ponies grazing on its banks. In the distance lay misty mountains. Closer were forests, green as emeralds. The sky was laced with birdsong. The flowers were busy with butterflies. And there, right beside the path, was a cherry tree, with pink petals strewn beneath.

Jakob had to close his eyes. He was so full of emotion—so dazzled by the splendor and the light—he knew he would cry if he gazed any longer. With his eyes closed, he was able to steady his breathing and calm himself down. He sat quite still for several minutes, then dared to wonder whether it was all a dream. *Perhaps I'll wake up,* he thought, *and find myself on Hamelin Hill, with nowhere to go but home.*

Suddenly he was scared to open his eyes. What if it all disappeared? But he could smell roses . . . and there were no roses on his side of Hamelin Hill.

Jakob dared to open his eyes. The glory was still there.

He had found it. He was in Paradise.

PART
FOUR

CHAPTER
THIRTY-THREE

Marianna sat down on her haunches, lifted a back leg, and violently scratched her ear.

"Flamin' fleas," she grumbled. "They're getting everywhere."

She stopped scratching and wondered what she could do to get rid of them. Scratching wasn't working, nor was rolling in dirt. But she hadn't tried water.

She sniffed the air. There was water ahead. On the far side of the meadow, under the trees. She padded over.

Oh, what a place! It was a deep pool, ringed by alders. Cool, still . . . Perfect for swimming, especially on a hot afternoon like this. Marianna started to wade in.

The water rose up her legs to the top of her haunches. That was far enough. She didn't want to float; she wanted to sit with her body right under the water. She eased herself down. Oh! That felt good! The water was soothing her tired feet and, better still, she could feel the fleas panicking. Soon they were jumping from her body. She could see them floating in the water like blackberry seeds: shiny dots, fat with blood.

She dipped her head under the water and held it there, shaking it from side to side to make sure she would be rid of them all. Then she rose to the surface again and looked at the water. There were clouds of dead bodies now, swirling like a sky full of starlings. And suddenly she remembered Hamelin. The river Weser, black and still, bloated with rats. The Piper, elegant in turquoise and jade, shimmering with life in a mire of death.

Marianna dipped her head underwater again and washed away all thoughts of him. Then she waded deeper and started swimming, rolled onto her back like an otter, and floated still, gazing at the trees overhanging the pool. *Jakob would love this*, she thought. *Perfect peace and no one watching.*

Ah, Jakob. She couldn't think about him without feeling guilty. She should have stayed with him. Looked after him. *Heaven knows who's looking after him now*, she thought. *It won't be Papa, that's for sure. He can't look after himself, let alone anyone else. Poor Jakob. I hope he's all right.*

Marianna closed her eyes and floated on, determined to enjoy the moment. She didn't have many good moments these days; it was hard to forget she was a fox. But here in the pool, with the dappled sunshine on her face and the quiet of the countryside enfolding her, she could almost believe she was a girl again.

Then her belly started rumbling. Not a polite, girly rumble but a long, low moan. *Feed me. Feed me now!* Marianna sighed and reluctantly opened her eyes. Sometimes she felt enslaved, like a genie in a lamp. As soon as her fox body called her, she had to obey.

It was calling her now. *Let's go hunting!*

CHAPTER
THIRTY-FOUR

Marianna headed for a busy rabbit warren that lay south of her home. She had hunted there several times since settling in the area and had always been successful.

Marianna's home was a huge oak tree. It had toppled in a storm many moons ago and now its trunk was perfectly hollow, warm and dry. Marianna had been overjoyed to find it. She had been wandering for more than a week, managing to survive, when one day she asked herself why she was constantly traveling. Where was she going? Round and round in circles, it seemed. Hamelin Hill was as close as it had ever been.

She had given up any hope of returning home or regaining her human form, so wandering made no sense. Here, there—it made no difference. She would still be a fox. She simply had to make the best of things. That was what she had been taught in life and it had been a hard lesson. The family had little to make the best of.

But it had been a useful lesson and it probably

explained how she had managed to survive. She had adapted and worked with her body where others might have fought against it. It didn't please her to do so. She felt dirty all the time and missed being able to wash her hands. If she wanted to clean herself, she had to use her tongue. It was horrible. She had to *lick her own backside clean*. It had to be done or things got worse. But she couldn't help feeling it was a disgusting habit. Her old dog, Scruff, had done it every day. She had scolded him. Told him to stop. But now she understood why he had done it. He didn't want to; he *had* to.

Food was a constant problem. In the beginning she had scavenged, eating anything she could find. Dead birds, eggs, worms, scraps thrown out by the elf farms. Then she had started stealing chickens. That had been scary. She was worried that the elves might catch her and turn her into a toad. A fox was bad enough, but a toad? *Eurgh!*

She wasn't proud of stealing chickens, but she knew it was her fox's instinct, working to keep her alive. And it was that same instinct that made her crave meat. Scavenged food filled her belly, but it left her sluggish. She needed strength and energy to survive. There was no escaping it—what she really needed was a supply of fresh rabbit meat.

Marianna's first attempt at killing a rabbit had gone wildly wrong—in a way she could never have imagined.

She had noticed a small warren on her travels and waited until dusk. That was something she had learned early on about rabbits: they fed mostly at dawn and dusk. By day, they stayed underground in their burrows.

So Marianna had waited till the sun was setting, then skirted around the back of the warren and hidden herself beneath a mulberry bush. She knew the rabbits mustn't see her or catch her scent on the wind. That was the fox again, taking over her senses. Twitching her nose and pricking her ears. Narrowing her eyes, lowering her haunches.

Rabbit!

The smell hit her hard and strong and she began to drool. She couldn't help it; her belly sensed a meal coming. She swallowed the saliva down and opened her mouth to breathe more easily. Her long pink tongue poked between her canine teeth, in and out in the rhythm of her breathing.

She peered through the bush. A lone rabbit was hopping toward her. It looked nervous. It wasn't grazing—just looking around, trying to sense danger. But it wasn't doing a good job of it. Marianna was within killing distance and still it came closer.

Something snapped inside Marianna. She sprang from the bush, landed on top of the rabbit, and sank her teeth into the scruff of its neck.

"Oh!" cried the rabbit. "Don't kill me! Please don't kill me!"

Marianna got such a fright, she dropped the rabbit and fell backward. "I won't," she stammered. "I promise."

She looked at the rabbit. It was a tiny scrap of a thing, all wet around the neck where her teeth and tongue had been. It was shaking and breathing so fast, Marianna thought it would faint.

"Thank you," it whispered.

Marianna took a deep breath to calm herself. Her heart was hammering like a woodpecker. "You gave me such a fright," she said at last. "I didn't think rabbits could talk."

"They can't," said the rabbit. "Not in this language. There's only me."

Marianna stared at it, horrified. A terrible thought was forming in her mind. She could hardly bear to say it out loud, but she did. "Are you from Hamelin?"

The rabbit nodded.

"Oh my!" cried Marianna. She had nearly killed one of the others. *Eaten* one of the others. She was as bad as the Beast.

"Who are you?" she asked.

"Lise Soliman," replied the rabbit.

"Soliman?" said Marianna. "Did your family make candles? On Jetty Lane?"

"Yes!" cried the rabbit. "I'm Lise! The eldest!"

"Quite tall?" asked Marianna. "Blonde hair— usually in braids?"

"That's me," said Lise proudly.

"Dear Lord," said Marianna. "I nearly ate you."

The rabbit sighed. "Would that have been so dreadful? Last night I went to sleep and prayed I'd never wake up again. It's not so bad for you— you're a fox. You'll survive. But I'm a rabbit. I'm someone's supper. I spend half my time looking over my shoulder. There are foxes and wolves and dogs and wildcats and who knows what else."

"Eagles?" said Marianna. "Hawks? Crows?"

"Oh, thank you very much," said Lise. "Now I have to watch the sky too."

"I'm sorry," said Marianna. "I wasn't thinking."

"No, you weren't," said the rabbit glumly. "You were too busy thinking about eating me."

"I'm sorry," said Marianna again. "I can't help it. But I promise you—I'll move on. I'll never hunt here again."

The rabbit smiled. "Really? Oh, I'm so glad, because I'd like to stay here. It's quiet and comfortable, and the other rabbits have made me very welcome. I'm even starting to understand their language! I feel like I've found a home."

Marianna grudgingly returned the smile. She felt cold and empty and envious. She was on her own. Wandering. Lost. But that wasn't Lise's fault.

Marianna took a deep breath and tried to sound cheerful. "Well, it's been lovely meeting you, Lise," she said, "but it's time I was moving on. I don't think we'll ever meet again so . . . good-bye! And good luck."

"Wait!" said Lise. "You haven't told me who *you* are."

"I'm Marianna, the shoemaker's daughter. From Leather Lane. I have a brother, Jakob."

"Oh, yes! I know who you are! Is Jakob not with you? I saw him on the walk."

Marianna shook her head. "He was left behind."

"Lucky him!"

Lise started to clean her long velvety ears. "My brother was turned into a weasel. I tried to speak to him but he ran away. Just as well, really. I think weasels eat rabbits if they're hungry enough. Oh, Marianna—before you go, there's something I should show you. You might want it."

The rabbit led Marianna to the front of the warren. Instantly there was a flurry of white tails as a dozen rabbits disappeared underground. But there was one left lying on the grass, ominously still.

"It's dead," said Lise, "but only just. I saw it happen. It wasn't sick—it was wounded. Must have been caught in a trap or something. It managed to get back here but then it just . . . died."

Marianna padded over to it. The rabbit was still warm. It almost looked asleep except its eyes were wide open. Marianna sniffed it and instantly the drooling began again. Her tongue appeared. She licked her lips and started to shake. She was going to eat it. Now that the rabbit was under her nose, she couldn't control the urge.

"Lise," she said, her voice coming out strangely hoarse and tight. "Don't watch."

"Don't worry," said Lise with a shiver. "I have no intention of doing so."

Lise turned away, so she saw nothing. But she heard the snarl and the snap, and smelled the blood, fresh in the air. And she suddenly felt glad that she wasn't a fox. It seemed such a savage, messy way to be.

That had been two weeks ago. Marianna had walked away from Lise determined to make a better life for herself. She would find a home and try to enjoy the world around her. She would explore her extraordinary new senses and practice using them until she was the best fox in Elvendale. In time, she might meet another fox. And it might be a he . . . and he might like her . . . and she might have a family. Cubs! How amazing that would be.

But for now, Marianna sat in the shadows, watching the rabbit warren. She was shivering a little—her fur was still damp from the swim—but it was wonderful to be free of fleas.

She tensed. The sun was dipping behind the far mountains. The rabbits would be out soon.

Aha! There was the first! A young buck, sniffing

the wind. Then came another and another. But Marianna waited. *Patience!* That was something else she had learned as a fox. If she attacked too soon, the rabbits would dive for their holes and she would catch nothing. If she bided her time, one would wander in her direction.

Marianna waited. She was in no hurry. And soon enough, a doe came her way. Plump and juicy! Marianna licked her lips, prepared to spring and—

DOOMF!

A man fell to the ground right in front of her, landing with such an almighty thump he nearly knocked himself out. Marianna had only seen him at the last minute: a great black shape appearing from the other side of the warren, waving his arms like a bird scarer. He had chosen a likely rabbit, chased it, fallen over *another* rabbit—and crashed to the ground like Marianna's oak.

Marianna glared at the man, her eyes hot with anger and vulpine disgust. A human! An oafish, clumsy human! Ruining everything she had carefully planned. And he was so dirty! Why didn't he clean himself, the filthy beggar? And why didn't he get up? He was just lying there like a stinking cow pie.

As Marianna watched, the man managed to raise himself up off the ground. He pushed his hair back from his face and looked around.

Marianna's eyes nearly fell out of her head.

"Dear Lord!" she yelped. "Papa!"

CHAPTER THIRTY-FIVE

Moller jumped at the sound of Marianna's voice and ducked, as if something might be thrown in his direction. "Who's there?"

Marianna emerged from the shadows. Immediately her father grabbed a rock and prepared to throw it at her.

"NO!" cried Marianna. "PAPA! It's me. Marianna."

The rock fell to the ground, along with Moller's lower jaw. He stared at her wildly, not wanting to believe his eyes. But he had seen the fox's lips move. Heard the voice, familiar yet different.

"Are you sure?" he said.

Marianna let out a deep sigh. Elvendale hadn't worked any magic on her father, it seemed. He was as stupid as ever.

"Of course I'm sure," she said. "I'm under an enchantment."

"Who did this to you?" he said, suddenly getting angry. "Tell me."

"Why?" said Marianna. "So you can punch him?"

Moller didn't reply, just turned away. He couldn't bear Marianna's hot gaze.

"It was the Piper," said Marianna at last.

"Did you do something to annoy him?"

"No!" cried Marianna. She was starting to feel angry now. Why did he always assume she was to blame?

"Then why did he do it?"

"I don't know," said Marianna. "It wasn't just me—he turned everyone into animals. He was angry and upset and didn't want us anymore. It was awful. We didn't see it coming."

Moller shrugged. "He's an elf."

"We didn't know that."

"I did," said Moller.

Marianna stared at him scornfully. "How could you know? And why didn't you say so, back in town? Why didn't you try to stop him?"

"I was . . . elsewhere at the time."

"Oh really? I can't guess where that was." Marianna sighed. She was growing tired of the conversation and the company. "What are you doing here?" she asked wearily. "I can't believe you came for me."

"No, I didn't," admitted her father. "I came for Jakob."

"*What?*"

"He's here," said Moller. "At least, I think he's here. Either that or he's run away from home."

"I don't understand," said Marianna in a fluster. "He didn't make it. I saw the door closing and he—"

"—was left behind. As usual."

"I thought he was with me," said Marianna. "If I'd realized, I'd—"

"It wasn't your fault," said Moller, unexpectedly letting her off the hook. "It was the Piper. You were enchanted then as you are now."

"But how did Jakob manage it? We came through a magic door. It was the only one."

"No," said Moller. "There are dozens of them. Jakob must have gotten lucky."

Marianna wondered how her father knew about elf doors, but she didn't ask. There were more important things.

"How long has he been here?" she asked. "Have you seen any sign of him? Has anyone told you anything?"

"Since last night," said Moller. "And no. I've spoken to no one."

"He could be anywhere," she said, beginning to fret. "I've got to find him. There's danger here."

"For some," agreed Moller darkly.

"There's a beast," said Marianna, not hearing him. "A terrible thing."

"You've seen it?"

148

"Yes," said Marianna. "It's the Piper. I saw him change."

Moller's eyes grew wide. "This is bad, Mari," he said, shaking his head. "I don't understand that Piper. Elves can be spiteful creatures, I know, but to steal you all away like that . . . It was a strange business."

"He was looking for a special child," said Marianna. "He said someone in Hamelin had magic powers but didn't know it. That's who he wanted. He made us touch a stone to find out who it was. So we did, but nothing happened, and that's when he flew into a rage and changed us all into animals. Except Karl. He *killed* him."

"Heaven help us," said Moller, hauling himself to his feet. "We've got to find Jakob." He started for the lane.

Marianna ran after him. She had heard something in her father's voice she wouldn't have believed possible: fear. Cold, urgent fear. "Why?" she asked. "What's wrong?"

"Jakob's the one he's looking for," said Moller.

"He can't be!" said Marianna. "He has no magic powers."

"He might," said Moller. "It's possible."

"How?" Marianna overtook her father and stopped him in his tracks. "Why do you say that?"

"You don't need to know."

"I do, Papa! Tell me."

Moller shook his head and carried on walking.

Marianna seized hold of his britches and pulled hard.

"Let go, Mari!"

She hung on harder and gave her best growl for good measure.

"Mari, let go!"

She shook her head from side to side like a dog with a rat.

"Mari!"

Moller kicked out so hard, Marianna was thrown through the air. She landed with a crunch in the lane, picked herself up, and glared at him with hateful eyes.

"I'm sorry, Mari," said Moller. "I didn't mean to do that. Come here."

He genuinely meant it, Marianna could tell, but she didn't go to him. What was he planning to do? Pat her like a puppy?

Moller sighed, looked for a boulder, and sat down heavily. "I'll tell you," he said. "Though I promised your mother I wouldn't."

Marianna went cold. What was this? A secret?

"It's possible Jakob has magic powers because of your mother," said Moller. "She . . . she . . ."

"What?"

"She . . . wasn't like us."

"What do you mean?" said Marianna, coming closer. "What was wrong with her?"

"Oh, there was nothing wrong," said Moller, and

he must have pictured her, because he suddenly smiled. His whole face softened. Marianna hadn't seen him like that in years.

"So—why?" asked Marianna.

"Because . . . she was an elf maiden."

Marianna stared at her father. She couldn't believe what he had just said.

"What?"

"It's true," said Moller. "This was her real home. Elvendale."

Marianna shook her head. A perfect image of her mother floated before her. A beautiful heart-shaped face. Green eyes. Gorgeous long hair, red as a fleeing fox. Marianna could remember her so clearly. Her smile. Her laughter, light as summer rain. The pain in her eyes when she lay dying. Why hadn't she said anything, even then?

"You're wrong," said Marianna. "You're lying."

"No," said Moller. "Why would I? And think about it, Mari. How else would I know how to get in here? Or know it's called Elvendale?"

"People talk. You could have heard something."

"Oh, grow up, Mari! Hear the truth. Stop arguing with me, girl, for once in your life." He rose to his feet and walked on.

Marianna sat in the lane, trying to make sense of the truth, if that was what it was. She desperately wanted proof. She tried to remember things her mother had done that seemed impossible. Magical. But she couldn't think of anything. And if she *was* an elf, why had she died so easily? So young? It was only a fever and elves lived for hundreds of years. Hadn't Mama said so?

And if her mama was an elf, didn't that make her half elf too? Just like Jakob? Did *she* have magical powers? No. She had touched the Standing Stone and nothing had happened. But then again, back in the caves with the Piper, she did seem to be the only one who felt something was wrong. She didn't seem to be under the enchantment all the time, like the others were. Perhaps that was a sign she was different? Maybe. But what about Jakob? Did he really have extraordinary powers, like the Piper said? Did he know? Had he hidden something from her?

It had grown dark. Her father was still storming down the lane; she could barely see him. Where was he going? *He has no idea,* thought Marianna bitterly. *He never will. He's useless—utterly useless at everything he does. If Jakob needs rescuing, heaven help him if Papa's his only hope.*

Marianna glanced at the sky. The moon was rising behind the mountains, round and yellow like a cheese. Nearly full.

Nearly full.

With a jolt, she remembered the night of the Beast. She closed her eyes and saw it again. The Beast, on the mound by the Standing Stone, silhouetted against the sky, howling at the moon. The full moon. She saw its eyes and its teeth and . . . Karl.

Jakob!

Instantly she was running. Down the lane, past her father, running to find Jakob before the Beast did.

"Mari!"

How long did she have? Two days? Three at most.

"MARI! WAIT!"

She heard her father's call but she didn't stop. Saving Jakob was her job. *Hers.* She didn't need her father. Never had, never would. Let him call! Call and shout till he croaked like a frog. She didn't care. She wasn't going back.

CHAPTER
THIRTY-SIX

Marianna ran through the night, barely aware of the countryside she was passing. Her head was whirling with questions, her heart was hurting with untold secrets—and her belly was still demanding dinner. So when an unwary rabbit suddenly crossed her path, Marianna seized and killed it before she realized what she was doing.

"Oh!" she said, looking at the limp brown body on the ground before her. "You poor thing. You didn't deserve that."

She picked the rabbit up gently, found a comfortable place to sit, and started to eat it. She didn't want to, but she knew her body would give her no peace if she didn't. And in a way, wasting the rabbit would be even worse than killing it. Then it would have died for nothing. So she started to pull off the fur and turned her mind to other things.

Marianna didn't know what had upset her most: the shock of seeing her father, the thought of Jakob being in danger, or the terrible family secret she had learned. It was probably the secret, she decided. That had turned her whole world upside down. Her mother had trusted her to look after Jakob. Why hadn't she trusted her with the truth?

Marianna's thoughts started to drift . . . Over the fields and the rivers, the woods and the streams. Over Hamelin Hill and on to the town. Over the rooftops and into the street where she had lived. Into the house and the attic room, where her own life had begun and her mother's life was ending. Marianna could see her lying there, in a shaft of sunlight, her soul fluttering in her breath like a trapped butterfly. And Marianna could see herself, at eight years old, holding her mother's hand, face wet with tears, leaning forward to catch her last words.

"Promise me, Mari," whispered her mother, "you'll look after Jakob. And your father. Whatever happens."

"I promise," said Marianna. She felt her hand being squeezed, one last time.

"You're strong, Mari. Always remember that. Simen?"

Moller stepped out of the shadows. He was holding Jakob by the hand.

Marianna stood up and let her father take her place. He gave her Jakob. She took her brother's hot little hand in her own and vowed never to let it go.

"Protect them, Simen," said her mother. "Love

them. Fight for them." Her voice faltered. She closed her eyes.

Her father leaned in very close. Her mother said something Marianna couldn't hear. Then he sat back, and Marianna saw a smile on her mother's face. Then she gasped—a soft, whispery intake of breath that sounded surprised, not pained—and her eyes opened one more time. And they seemed to be seeing something *wonderful*, as if the room had suddenly filled with rainbows or bright butterflies. Marianna longed with all her heart to see the vision too. To share this magical moment with her mother. But it was fading. Her mother's eyes were closing, and already the world seemed darker without them.

One last sigh, then it was over.

And Moller let out a wail of such anguish that Marianna, back in Elvendale, was truly shocked. She hadn't remembered that. She saw him fall upon the bed, his sobs coming thick and fast and unstoppable. And it was several minutes before he rose unsteadily to his feet, walked over to the tiny attic window, and opened it. Then he gazed out, over the rooftops, to Hamelin Hill beyond. And only now did Marianna understand why he had done that. It was as if her mother's soul had indeed left her as a butterfly and he was setting it free. Watching it go, beginning the long journey home to Elvendale.

Marianna chewed the rabbit and thought on. That afternoon in the attic . . . That was when everything began to change in the house. Her father had tried to cope, but it was all too much for him. The days became weeks, the weeks became months, and he fell apart like a worn-out coat. His temper frayed. His life unraveled. He burst at the seams: he was so full of emotion. Soon he was nothing but a shabby rag of a man, no good to anyone.

Promise me, Mari, you'll look after Jakob. Whatever happens. What had Mama meant by that? *Whatever happens.* Marianna hadn't thought about it before, but now she had to wonder. Did her mother fear this might happen? Did she know that someone might come searching for Jakob?

"I *have* looked after him," said Marianna hotly, through a mouthful of rabbit. "I have, Mama! I have done my best, for three years, and it's been hard. Really hard, but I've done it. And I'm sorry I didn't wait for him at the door. I should have kept him closer. But if I had, he'd be dead now, Mama, so it was all for the best. And I *will* find him again, I promise. Now I know he's here, I will find him and keep him safe forever."

Marianna finished the rabbit. She ran her tongue around her lips to tidy herself up, then rubbed her muzzle against her leg, just to be sure. She sighed. She couldn't lie to herself anymore. There was one promise she hadn't kept. Three little words she had chosen to forget over the years. *And your father.* That was what her mother had truly said. *Promise me, Mari, you'll look after Jakob. And your father. Whatever happens.* She had known, hadn't she? She had known that her husband would crumble without her, and it would fall to Mari to look after him. *You're strong, Mari. Always remember that.*

Yes, she was strong. Her father was weak but she was a survivor. That was why there was food in her belly while he had none.

That was why she had to go back.

Moller sat on a log, catching his breath. He had walked so hard, he had given himself a cramp. He was hot, he was tired, he was hungry, and he longed for a drink. He wouldn't deny it. Oh, but the look on Marianna's face . . . Even through fox fur, he had seen her disgust. And she was right. Look at him! Dirty, smelly, and drunk. That's how she remembered him, and he hadn't changed.

"But I *must*," he told himself. "Jakob needs me now and I'm no use to him as I am. Get a grip on yourself, man. Be strong for once in your life. Like Mari."

He started. There was a sound. *Pad, pad, pad*, coming toward him down the lane. He held his breath, hardly daring to hope.

Marianna. It had to be. There was a fox coming right toward him with something swinging from its jaws. A freshly killed rabbit. Moller felt his heart lurch with unexpected joy.

"Mari!" he cried. "Mari!"

Marianna dropped the rabbit at his feet.

"Yes, Papa," she said. "It's me. And this is your supper."

CHAPTER
THIRTY-SEVEN

While Moller was cooking his supper, Jakob was settling down on a bed of leaves. In truth, father and son weren't that far apart, but Jakob had no idea his father was nearby, while Moller couldn't begin to guess his son's location. All he could do was hope that Jakob was safe and not too hungry.

Jakob wasn't hungry at all. He had enjoyed the best day of his life and it had ended with a delicious and unexpected feast.

He had spent the morning strolling along green lanes, delighting in the warmth of the day and the gorgeous countryside around him. He had swung his staff to knock the heads off thistles, whistled like a blackbird, picked handfuls of berries from hedges, and sat awhile to savor them. There was no hurry to him at all.

He loved his new legs. He had never imagined that walking could be so exhilarating. Back in Hamelin, he had been friendly with a peddler. Konrad sold ribbons and lace from a basket. He walked all over the country, from town to town, village to village, and often talked about "the freedom of the open road." That had puzzled Jakob. He couldn't imagine how it would feel to walk for hours, days, weeks. But now he knew exactly what Konrad had meant. Being able to walk was a glorious gift. And with all his heart, he prayed that it would never be taken away from him.

By early afternoon, when the sun was at its highest, Jakob found a shady spot beneath some trees and enjoyed a nap. Then he walked on through the changing landscape. It started to look cultivated rather than wild. There were fields instead of meadows and the hedgerows were well tended. Then he heard an unmistakable lowing.

Jakob stood on his tiptoes, looked over a hedge, and found a whole herd of cows. Beautiful, pure-black cows with red ears and red tasseled tails. Spiral horns tied with ribbons. Ruby hooves and long-lashed eyes. Black udders, heavy with milk.

But there was something strange about the herd. There were silver buckets beneath some of the udders and, though no one was visibly milking the cows, milk was squirting out in creamy streams and landing with a satisfying *slosh* in the pails below.

When the udders were dry, the buckets picked themselves up and moved on to the next cow, where the squirting and sloshing began all over again.

"That's amazing!" whispered Jakob, wishing

Marianna was there to see it with him. "It's magic!"

He walked along the lane to the next field. Here there was wheat, long and ripe, swaying seductively in the warm summer breeze.

Jakob became aware of a sound: *sssssssip, sssssssip!* Through the field came a trio of silver scythes, slicing through the cornstalks. *Sssssssip, sssssssip!* No one was holding them. The grinning scythes were working alone. *Sssssssssip, sssssssip, sssssssip!*

Jakob was intrigued. "The farm can't be completely worked by invisible hands," he reasoned. "There must be *someone* here."

He was right. In the next field he found the farmer.

This field was a clover meadow, busy with bees that flew from one pink flower to the next. In a corner stood the beehives, but they weren't plain wooden boxes like the ones around Hamelin Town. Each beehive was beautifully carved and brightly painted—a home fit for a queen.

Beside the beehives stood an elf, and Jakob was amazed to see that he wasn't wearing any protective clothing. He had often watched the Hamelin beekeepers at work. They wore thick padded suits and hats with veils, and they always pumped smoke into the hives to clear the bees before they removed the honeycombs.

But this elf had neither smoke nor padding. He

was removing the honey with his bare hands and the bees weren't bothering him at all. They seemed to be giving the honey willingly.

As Jakob watched, the elf removed the last of the honey from a hive. Then he did a curious thing. He bowed deeply, said some words Jakob couldn't hear, reached into his pocket, and brought something out. Jakob couldn't see what it was—it was too small. But whatever it was, the elf slipped it into the hive. Then he bowed again and moved on to the next one.

Jakob was drooling. The honey looked delicious and he was hungry. He smacked his lips and moved on down the lane.

Soon he came to the farm buildings: a jumble of sheds and shelters, barns and pens, with the farmhouse set a little way behind. Jakob's eyes were particularly drawn to a long, low stone barn. It had a turf roof and a wooden door, and he couldn't help wondering what was inside. So he slipped across the farmyard, opened the door, and went in.

"Aha! Goodies!"

Inside the barn there were two enormously long tables, one on each side, laden with wicker baskets. On one table the baskets were full of nuts: almonds, walnuts, acorns, hazelnuts, and a dazzling array of unfamiliar ones. On the other table the baskets were full of berries: red, yellow, orange. Bright as beads.

Countless more berries had been threaded onto strings. They hung from the roof rafters like hundreds of necklaces.

"Oh!" sighed Jakob. "Mari would *love* one of those." He started to walk the length of the barn, wondering how he could get one down. And he was so busy thinking, he didn't see the elf children until he nearly trod on them. He heard a warning *"Aa-lo!"* and a giggle and, when he looked down, he saw two smiling faces. A girl and a boy, sitting on the floor, threading more berries.

"Sorry!" said Jakob. "I didn't see you there! I was looking at the strings."

The elf children didn't reply, just kept on smiling. Then the girl put down her needle and thread, rose to her feet, and fetched a neat wooden tray from one of the tables. She offered it to Jakob.

There were pale brown cubes on the tray. Some kind of sweetmeat? Jakob took a piece and popped it into his mouth.

Mmm! Almond and honey.

He took another, then another. Soon he had eaten every piece, but the elf children didn't seem to mind. They laughed and pointed to their bellies.

"Yes," said Jakob. "It's good. Very good!" He grinned. His teeth were sticky with sweet stuff. The elf children clapped in delight. Then the girl said something to her brother. He nodded and they both ran past Jakob and out of the barn.

"Oops!" said Jakob. "Was it something I said?"

He didn't have time to ponder. Suddenly the door opened and there stood the farmer.

"Oh dear," said Jakob. He felt like he had back in the caves—cold and panicky. His heart was pounding and his throat felt tight. Had he done something wrong? Did they think he had come to steal something?

He glanced around, desperately looking for some means of escape. But there was no other door. He had walked into a trap.

The elf stepped inside and studied Jakob with a cool, green, silent gaze. Then he reached into a wooden crate, brought out a rough piece of cloth, and laid it flat on the table.

Jakob was horrified. The elf was going to gag him. Tie him up!

Or was he?

To Jakob's surprise, the elf began to select nuts and berries. A handful of this, a handful of that. All went onto the cloth. Then he pulled a piece of string from his pocket, gathered the cloth into a bundle, and tied it.

The elf children reappeared, carrying a basket full of brown-paper packages. They skipped the length of the barn, beamed at Jakob, and offered him the basket. Jakob stood there bewildered. Then the adult stepped forward, casually tossed the bundle of berries into the basket—and smiled. It was so fleeting, Jakob wondered if he had imagined it. But then the elf nodded and he was sure. He nodded in return and took the basket.

"Thank you," he said. "Thank you very much."

The elves stepped aside and invited Jakob to leave. And he was nearly out of the door when he remembered something.

"Oh!" he said, spinning around. "May I . . . ?" He pointed at the berry necklaces dangling from the roof. "For my sister."

The elf nodded, reached for a pointed stick, and unhooked one of the strings. He laid it gently in the basket. Jakob was thrilled. It was exactly the one he wanted. The shiny red berries were the same shade as Marianna's hair.

"Thank you," he said. "She'll be thrilled."

With a smile and a wave, Jakob left the farm and carried on down the lane. As he walked, he asked himself why he had felt so scared in the barn.

"There's nothing to be frightened of here," he told himself. "It's a heavenly place and the elves are friendly. I bet *everything* is friendly! Dogs won't bite and bees won't sting. Ants won't steal your food. No, they'll *bring* you food! A whole army of ants will bring you supper, carrying it in the air over their heads. Fifty of them carrying an apple! A thousand of them struggling with a round of cheese!"

He laughed at the picture he had painted and

walked on. Eventually he reached a widening in the lane with a pond and a warm mossy bank beside it. It was a perfect place for a picnic.

"Ooh!" he said, as he collapsed onto the grass. "My legs are *tired*! They're not used to walking like this." He started to unpack the elves' basket.

"Cakes!" he cried, carefully unwrapping the first of many enticing parcels. "Cheese . . . butter . . . soft bread rolls . . . something pink—" He sniffed the package. "I have no idea what this is, but it smells good! Pears . . . milk! From those magic cows! Peaches . . . nuts and berries . . . and a pot of honey. What a feast!"

Jakob had eaten his unexpected supper, walked on till sunset, then found the spot where he chose to sleep. And as he curled up on his bed of leaves, he couldn't help wishing—for the second time that day—that Marianna was there beside him, sharing the adventure. She would have loved the magical cows. And she would be so thrilled with his new body! She would make him walk up and down, turn around, touch his toes—until she was convinced he really was better. Then she would smile at him, her eyes would go all crinkly, and she would look like she was going to cry—just a tear or two—because she was so happy for him.

I wonder where she is, he thought. *Where did the Piper*

take her? And what are they all doing now? I bet they're having such fun.

With that thought, he sank into a deep, dreamy sleep. The Piper played a merry tune and Marianna followed him, wearing her berry necklace. Jakob followed her, dancing like a fool on a feast day. They danced to the top of Hamelin Hill, caught hold of the clouds, and raced across the sky, then slid to earth on a shimmering rainbow. Tumbling, tumbling onto leaves, into sleep and on till morning.

CHAPTER
THIRTY-EIGHT

Jakob awoke to another warm, dry day. He breakfasted on a bread roll and a piece of cheese he had saved from the night before, then washed his face in a nearby stream and strolled on.

But the day didn't seem as bright as the one before, nor the world so wonderful. Yes, the sun was out, shining like a happy pancake in the great blue skillet of the sky. And yes, there were extraordinary things to see, like strawberry trees and sheep with wings and mushrooms that moved, walking in lines, one behind the other like mountain goats.

But Jakob had no one to share his wonder with. He was alone. And that was a cruel joke, because now, with his fine new legs, there was no reason for him to be left out anymore. "Bring me a gang of boys," he said, "and I'll run with the fastest of them! Take me to the river and I'll show you how to swim, faster than a salmon. Bring the girls too! Let them watch. They won't shame me now."

Where *were* they, Marianna and the others? Where

had the Piper taken them? Jakob pondered this, mile after mile. Could he find them? Maybe, maybe not. He certainly had nothing to lose by trying.

There an old man, back in Hamelin, who sat outside the abbey most days. Jakob liked to sit with him because he told wonderful stories. Tales of bold knights and daunting dragons. Luscious ladies and hideous hags. Now, thinking back, Jakob remembered something important. The knights traveled all over the land but they always had a quest—a task, a challenge—something they had to do. They didn't wander aimlessly. They always knew where they were going. And if an adventure happened along the way—a lady needed rescuing from a tower, say, or an evil knight needed to be challenged—they would welcome it. They would do whatever had to be done, then return to their quests.

That's what he needed. A quest. And he had one, didn't he? *Sir Jakob and the Quest of the Missing Children*—that was it! He even had his own magical equipment—because a knight always had something magical, whether it was a sword that would never break, a potion to help him breathe underwater, or boots that could walk through fire. Jakob had his staff with its marvelous globe. That was special—though Jakob didn't know exactly what it could do. It hadn't done anything magical as yet except glow in the dark.

Sir Jakob of the New Legs . . . That's who he was! But he needed a sword.

He left the path, rummaged under the nearest trees, and pulled out a fallen branch. No! That was too crooked. He found a straighter piece and snapped off the excess wood. Perfect! He tucked his new wooden sword under his belt. Now the adventure could begin!

CHAPTER
THIRTY-NINE

Jakob headed south, deeper into the country. Now that he had a quest, he was more alert to the sounds around him. He listened for any trace of music in the air. And he found it: in the rippling of a stream and the full-throated song of a thrush; in the rhythmic chopping of a woodcutter's ax; in the call of a curlew; in the hot drone of tawny bees; in the magical tinkling of harebells by the side of the lane. But he didn't hear a pipe or the patter of dancing feet.

The sun rose higher and the day began to bake. Jakob was walking between open fields and the low hedges gave no shade. He needed a drink, a meal, a rest, but could see no hope of getting them. Not unless he cut across the fields and headed for the forest.

The forest. It was vast, dark, forbidding—and out of his way. It would mean leaving the path. Or would it? Suddenly, as if by magic, he came to a parting in the lane. One path carried on ahead, the way he had been going. The other turned left, to the forest.

Jakob didn't have to think twice. He took the left-hand turn and headed down the new lane. Soon he knew he had made the right decision. The hedges grew higher, so the lane was shady. He passed a pond and was able to drink. The ground was soft and springy beneath his feet.

Then he heard it.

Laughter. High-pitched girly giggles, somewhere up ahead. Jakob stopped and listened hard. They sounded close. There were voices too. He couldn't make out what they were saying, but they didn't sound elven.

Jakob hurried on. When he came to a large flat stone, he scrambled onto it and peered all around. Looked to see whether he could get into the forest any quicker. He couldn't. He would have to wait till the end of the lane, but it wasn't far.

Jakob started to run, his feet pounding the soft earth.

"Let them be there," he panted. "Don't let me lose them this time." The memories were flooding back. The hillside. The closing door. Marianna's face, white as a candle. He ran harder, faster than he had run so far. Was that *pipe music* he could hear? Yes! Soft and insistent. Sweetly seductive.

He burst out of the lane like a cork from a bottle and stopped, gasping. He looked around. Listened again. The forest lay ahead of him. Still. Unmoving. Silent. Tunnels of trees. Stripes of sunlight and shadow.

Jakob felt panic thumping inside him like a horde of angry imps. The girls had gone. He had been close, *really* close, yet he had lost them.

"Stupid, stupid, *stupid!*" he raged. "You should have cut through the hedge."

"Ja-kob. Oh, Ja-kob!"

A voice, light as thistledown, floating between the trees.

Marianna?

"Ja-kob. Ja-kob!"

"MARIANNA?" Jakob peered between the trees. He could hear voices again. Boys' as well as girls'.

"Marianna! Is that you? Are you in there? Come out!"

Nothing.

Jakob wavered at the forest edge. He was overjoyed to have found Marianna and the others, and yet . . . something didn't feel quite right. Why wasn't Marianna coming out? It wasn't like her to tease him.

"Marianna? Come out. Please. I need to see it's you."

Silence. Jakob heard his heart beat, once, twice, then—

"Come on, Jakob. Play the game." A boy's voice. It sounded like Johann, the butcher's boy.

"There's nothing to be scared of." It was the girl's voice again. "Promise!"

Jakob made up his mind . . . took a deep breath . . . smiled bravely . . . and entered the Whispering Forest.

Behind him, in a flutter of fire-gold feathers, a hawk rose majestically into the sky, circled three times, and—*fffooo!*—it disappeared. Over the fields, over the meadows, over the wildwoods, back to Hamelin Hill.

PART
FIVE

CHAPTER
FORTY

Finn was lying on a couch, tending his wound. Despite the ferocious heat outside, his home was cool and shaded, and he was grateful for that. He was feverish enough without sunstroke making things worse.

The floor was strewn with bloody bandages and spilled water. A faint odor hung in the air: not unpleasant, but enough to attract flies. Finn had to dress the wound as swiftly as possible.

He worked with practiced hands, his thoughts unraveling along with the fresh bandage.

"I can't believe I'm facing this again," he said to himself. "The rats were there. The child was there, I know he was. I came *so close* to being cured! I still don't see why it went so badly. I did exactly what the stag told me to do. The curse should be gone, and instead . . ."

He tied the bandage and lay back against the couch. Closed his eyes to shut out the pain and despair. The children of Hamelin had been his last hope. Centuries of pain and waiting had all come to nothing. Now he didn't want to go on. He was fit and healthy. He could expect to live for hundreds of years. But did he want to? Alone, without a wife or family or friends? He could see nothing but loneliness, centuries of it, stretching into forever.

Foooomf! Flyte flew into the room faster than a slingshot.

"I have seen him!" cried the hawk. "The special child!"

"I don't think so," said Finn wearily. "I took every child, Flyte, and they all touched the stone. The special one wasn't there."

"He is now."

"What?"

"I have seen him. A boy. He is a Hamelin child—I remember him. Though he has changed. He was lame before. He isn't now."

Finn stared, openmouthed. "It must be him," he said at last. "His power is strengthening him, now that he's in Elvendale. But how did he get in here?"

"Does it matter?" said Flyte. "He is here. That is all you need to know."

"He's at the Standing Stone, you say?"

"No. That would be easy. He is in the worst place possible."

"The forest?"

The hawk nodded.

Finn took his head into his hands and closed his

eyes. He could feel himself growing cold, despite his raging fever. "Why?" he whispered. "Why does he have to be there? Have I not suffered enough?"

"Follow him," said Flyte.

"No," said Finn. "I cannot. Not into the forest."

"You must."

"I cannot!" cried Finn wildly. "Look at me, Flyte! The mere thought of going in there has reduced me to *this*." He held out trembling hands.

"You must conquer your fear," said Flyte. "You have everything to gain and nothing to lose—except your life. And I believe you care little for that these days."

Finn shook his head. He wasn't convinced.

"Think now," urged Flyte. "The boy is alone in the forest. You must find him before something else does."

Finn stared at Flyte: a dead, fish-eyed gaze.

"If that boy dies,'" said Flyte, "you will be cursed forever. Is that what you want?"

Finn stared on. Time seemed to be standing still. He could feel nothing but the throb of his wound.

"Well?" said Flyte. "Is it?"

Finn shook his head. He rose awkwardly to his feet and ran his fingers through his hair. The color had drained from his face. He felt hot, cold, and giddy all at the same time. But something had to be done.

"You're right," he said. "I have to find him."

"So," said the hawk, "what would you have me do?"

"Right now?" said Finn. "Find Aspen. The sooner we're there, the sooner it's over."

CHAPTER
FORTY-ONE

Jakob walked deeper into the forest. The laughter and voices had gone. Instead there were whispers drifting between the trees, fluttering like moths. He couldn't hear what they were saying, but he suspected they were talking about him. Deep in his heart, he knew he had made a terrible mistake. He shouldn't have entered the forest. Now he couldn't find the way out even if he wanted to. As soon as he had entered, the trees had closed in behind him.

"Remember who you are," he said to himself. "You're Sir Jakob of the New Legs. You have no fear of dragons or trolls or . . . whispering things. You can face any danger. Fight any foe."

He went on. After five minutes, he had convinced himself he really could face any challenge—which was fortunate, because he was just about to encounter one.

Jakob hardly noticed it at first. It was covered by a lattice of brambles. But there was something about the shape that made him curious. He pulled at the tangled stems and there, hidden underneath, was a well. A low, square, stone well with intricately carved sides. It was full to the brim with dark, still water.

Jakob was hot and thirsty. He put his lips to the water and started to drink. And as he did, a head appeared from the bottom of the well, silently rising up through the water until it bobbed on the surface like an apple.

Jakob fell back and stared in horror at the head. It was just a head, nothing more, with a face that was neither young nor old, male nor female—simply a bit of everything. A mass of tangled hair floated around it, slimy as pondweed. The lips were long and thin, like two slugs kissing. The eyes, when they opened, were gray as gravestones.

Slowly the thin lips moved and the head spoke.

"I am the Well of Wishes," it said, "and to anyone who finds me and drinks my water, I offer three wishes. Think carefully before you speak. Choose wisely now."

Jakob was speechless for a moment. Then he started to grin. "Well, this is a bit of luck!" he said at last. "Thank you for your offer—and your advice. I *will* think carefully—if I may have a few minutes?"

"You may have as long as you want," said the head. "I am in no particular hurry." The eyes closed. A ghost of a smile passed across its cold lips.

Jakob thought carefully. He knew what he wanted,

but he had to make sure he got things right. He didn't want to be like the man in Marianna's story who wished for a sausage and got it on the end of his nose.

"I wish—I could see my sister, Marianna," he said at last.

The gray eyes opened and the head nodded. "Watch," it said. And with that it started to sink back down into the water of the well. Then the water turned cloudy, like the sky when a storm is coming. But slowly it began to clear and Jakob could see a vision forming. There was a lane, overhung by trees, with a ditch running along one side . . . and then a man walked into the picture.

Jakob blinked in surprise. "That looks like Papa." He peered closer. "It *is* Papa! But where's Marianna?"

A fox came into the picture, trotting along the road at the man's heels. And as Jakob watched, the fox paused, turned, and looked straight at him. Its face grew bigger and bigger until it filled the well. Then the water went cloudy again. The vision disappeared and the head returned to the surface.

Jakob could hardly speak. "Was that Marianna?" he managed. "Was that her? The fox?"

The head nodded. "She has fallen under an enchantment."

"Is she here?" asked Jakob. "With my father?"

"So many questions," complained the head.

"I have to ask, otherwise I can't make my wishes," said Jakob. "You told me to choose wisely. That's what I'm trying to do."

Silence.

"Please," begged Jakob.

The head sighed: a sound that seemed to travel through time, collecting the boredom of endless centuries.

"Yes, yes, and yes," said the head. "She is here in Elvendale with your father."

Jakob thought for a moment. "Then I wish—Marianna could be here with me."

"Easily done," said the head. It puckered its lips and began to whistle.

Jakob could hardly hear it at first: the sound was incredibly high-pitched, like the call of a bat. But it seemed to work. Within seconds, he heard a patter of paws on the forest floor and a rich russet head appeared through the undergrowth.

"Mari?" he said. "Is that you?"

The fox cocked its head to one side and came closer. Jakob looked into its eyes, but he couldn't see any sign of his sister. Then he heard more pattering and a second fox appeared, then a third and a fourth. They all looked the same. Jakob started to get flustered. He couldn't choose. And he was just about to say, *I wish I could tell which one's Mari*, when he stopped himself, just in time.

"No!" he told himself. "There's only one wish

186

left! Don't waste it. You'll need it to change her back."

More and more foxes were arriving. There were dozens of them: red as apples, red as cherries, red as Christmas holly berries. But there was still no way of telling which was Marianna. He couldn't pick the friendliest—three were jumping up at him, trying to lick his face. One was sucking his fingers. Two were rubbing against his legs. Five were barking.

"Oh, I don't know what to do!" cried Jakob. "I want to help my sister, but I don't know if she's here. She might be miles away—and if I wish she was a girl again, she might change but never find me. It's quite a puzzle."

"Such is life," said the head.

Jakob fell to his knees before the well and looked straight into the pale eyes.

"Please," he said. "Please help me."

The eyes narrowed. "Comb me."

"What?"

"Comb me," said the head. "Comb out my hair. Make me pretty." A golden comb appeared on the well rim, glinting against the dark stone.

Jakob rolled up his sleeves and hauled the head out of the well. It was surprisingly heavy and the skin felt oily to the touch. Jakob sat down, took the head into his lap, picked up the comb, and started to untangle the matted hair.

The head purred with pleasure like a tabby cat.

"Wait until morning," it said in between purrs. "Your sister will be here by then."

"Can she be cured?" said Jakob. "Can the spell be broken?"

"Yes," said the head, "but first you must pick her out from all the other foxes. If you choose correctly, you can make the wish."

Jakob felt his heart sinking. "I *will* pick her out," he told himself. "I *must*. She can't be a fox for the rest of her life. I've got to save her."

Though how he was going to find Marianna with dozens of foxes to choose from, he couldn't begin to imagine.

CHAPTER
FORTY-TWO

Marianna was walking along a lane with her father when she heard the call. She stopped and sat down.

"What's the matter?" said Moller.

"I don't know," said Marianna. "I feel funny." She tilted her head and listened hard. "I can hear something—a whistle. It's calling me. I have to go."

"You can't," said Moller. "It could be the Ratcatcher."

"No—don't say that! It's bad enough I have to go."

Moller put his hands over her ears. "Don't listen to it."

"I can't help it," said Marianna, pulling away from him. "It's in my head. In my heart. I can feel it pulling me. I have to go."

Moller wrapped his arms around his daughter and was surprised to find she was trembling. "I won't let you go," he said. "We can fight this together. Try, Mari, try!"

"I *am* trying," snapped Marianna, starting to wriggle. "But it's too strong."

Moller tightened his grip. "I won't let you go, Mari. That Ratcatcher can whistle till sundown—he won't get you."

"Oh, yes, he will, if that's what he wants. You can't stop him. Why do you think you can save me now, Papa? You didn't save me last time."

"That's not fair, Mari."

"Isn't it?" She twisted in his arms and glared at him with her hazel eyes. "Where *were* you last time, anyway? Drunk in an alley? You were the only one who wasn't there. The *only* one. You didn't even try to save me."

"I'm trying now," said Moller, his face flushing with passion and exertion. "I'm here, aren't I?"

"You came for Jakob!" said Marianna. "You didn't come for me! You said so yourself."

"I couldn't come for you because I couldn't leave Jakob," said Moller. "I was torn, Mari. Torn in two. I had to decide who needed me more. And that was Jakob. You're strong, Mari. So strong you frighten me sometimes. You'll do whatever it takes. I can't stop you."

He had tears in his eyes—Mari saw them—though whether they were tears of anger or despair or love, she couldn't tell. She couldn't think straight any more. Every fiber of her being was urging her to run. Yes, she was strong—but she couldn't fight this.

Couldn't fight the Piper. Not on her own. She felt herself slipping from her father's grip. She started to panic. She didn't want to go. *She didn't want to go.* This time the Piper might break her completely. Her father was the only one standing between them.

"Papa!" she cried. "Don't let me go! Hold on!"

"I'm trying," said Moller, desperate now, "but there's something at work here. Some kind of magic. I don't think I can hold you much longer."

He was right. Marianna suddenly slipped from his grasp. She seemed to be bodily wrenched from him. Her legs started to move, taking her off down the lane at a fast run. Too fast for Moller to keep pace. With a great effort, she managed to turn her head and call over her shoulder. "Papa! Find me!"

"I will, Mari! I will!" Moller waved his arms wildly, staring after her, openmouthed, wretched, crushed.

He hoped she had heard him. She was running so fast, she was almost out of sight already. A smudge of red against the greenery of the lane.

Moller sank to his knees and took his head into his hands. His heart felt dry and twisted, like a wrung-out rag. He felt old, useless, and tired from the struggle. What on earth had possessed her? She had fought like a demon. He couldn't hold her.

"I've let you down again, Mari," he said. "God knows I tried, but I let you down again." He shook his head. "This can't keep happening. I promised your mother I'd look after you. Fight for you, protect you. *Pah!* A rotten job I've made of it so far." He raised his head and rubbed away a tear with the back of his hand. He gazed down the empty lane. "But it's not over till it's over, eh? Perhaps my time will come."

Moller rose wearily to his feet and started walking. And it wasn't long before his spirits began to rise. Soon he was striding down the lane, shoulders back, arms pumping, head held high. He even managed a smile.

"I'm coming, Mari," he said. "Don't you worry about that! I'm coming. And heaven help that Ratcatcher when I get there!"

CHAPTER
FORTY-THREE

Finn watched the Whispering Forest come closer. He didn't want to go there. He wanted to run in the opposite direction, but he wasn't the one doing the running. Aspen was thundering beneath him, his tail streaming out behind like a silken scarf. At least he was enjoying the journey.

Closer it came. Closer. Finn could imagine the trees starting to whisper, *He's coming! He's coming!* The rumor would reach the ears of the forest. The creatures, older than time, that lived in its dark heart—they would surely come for him. To enter the forest once was folly. To enter it twice was madness.

"I can't do it," he muttered. "I can't go in there."

Aspen snorted, gathered his strength and leaped over a high hedge. Then he turned abruptly and started racing down a green lane.

Finn suddenly had the feeling he had been there before.

"This is it," he said. "This is the way I came last

time." The memories flooded back. He could hear the hounds and the hunting horn. Feel the excitement and urgency of the hunt. He could almost believe the stag was there again, pounding down the lane to the forest, leading him to his destiny.

Then Aspen slowed to a trot and they were there, at the forest edge where it had all begun. Finn could hear Perlal's voice, warning him not to go any farther. Oh, how he wished he had heeded his friend's advice that day.

Finn dismounted and decided to sit awhile. He gazed into the forest and fancied he could see himself, many years younger, riding through the trees.

"How easily lives change," he mused. "One decision, made in a moment, and everything alters forever. What if I had listened to Perlal? Where would I be now? I would have ridden back with the others and feasted at Fennon's house. His sisters would have welcomed us. *Ah!* I might have married one of them. Armesia, with the amber eyes . . ."

He fell silent and sank into a whirlpool of ifs and maybes, spinning round and round in a tantalizing vision of what might have been. If only, if only . . .

It was the pain in his leg that pulled him back into reality. Nothing had changed. Aspen was still cropping the grass beside him. Flyte was perched on a gatepost, watching for mice. The forest lay still and cool in the heat of the day.

Finn clambered to his feet and stiffly walked

toward the forest. How peaceful it looked! How inviting! Today it was lush and green, and alive with the calls of unseen birds. The fringe was speckled with wood anemones, white as snowfall. This was a place that teased travelers with its beauty. Lured them in. Promised they would be welcome.

How untrue that was. No one was welcome in the Whispering Forest. No one was safe from its tricks and cruelty.

Finn stopped at the very edge of the forest. He couldn't go any farther. Suddenly he felt weak and fluttery, as if his body was made of butterflies. His lungs had to work harder and harder, just to keep a breath in his body.

He staggered to the nearest tree and put his arms around it. Clung on tight, as if the ground was about to disappear beneath his feet and sweep him into oblivion.

"How can I go in there like this?" he gasped. "How can I find the boy when I can't even stand upright?"

He tore himself away from the tree, stumbled toward the open land and collapsed in a heap on the grass.

Flyte joined him.

"I can't do it," said Finn despairingly. "I can't conquer the fear. When I reached the trees, my legs gave out. It's my second time, Flyte. My body knows it and won't let me enter."

195

"You have two bodies," said Flyte.

Finn stared at the hawk. "You think the Beast could do it?"

"Maybe, maybe not," said Flyte. "When the Beast takes your body, it takes your mind as well, does it not?"

Finn nodded. "More or less."

"Then you will lose your fear. The Beast has no fear. It has no memory of this forest; it has never been here. It is driven by one desire only—the desire to hunt. So tell it to hunt for the boy. Make that the last thought in your mind as it steals your body. *Find the boy.*"

Finn pondered the idea. "I think it will work," he said at last. "Flyte, do you realize what this means? I could be cured by morning!"

"Perhaps," said the hawk. "But first you must survive the night."

CHAPTER
FORTY-FOUR

Jakob awoke to find a large pink tongue licking his face.

"Mari?"

He struggled to sit up. The fox began to lick his arm, but Jakob knew it wasn't his sister. He didn't know *how* he knew; he just did. He rubbed his face with his hands, yawned, and rose to his feet. And that was when the enormity of the challenge hit him. The forest was full of foxes. Hundreds of them. Thousands of them. All the foxes in Elvendale were there: curled up into neat russet bundles; lying stretched out in warm pools of sunlight; play-fighting like cubs; cleaning one another's ears; barking at squirrels. How would he ever find Marianna?

Hope shriveled inside him like a snail in sunshine. He pushed his way through the furry throng and knelt in front of the well. Washed his face. Drank a cool, calming draught. As he did, the head rose from the murky depths and greeted him.

"So," it said, "are you ready to choose?"

"Yes," said Jakob. "I suppose I am. But I don't know how—or *why*, for that matter. Why do I have to choose? Why can't I just make my last wish?"

"Because there are rules in this forest," said the head. "Rules that must be obeyed. You have broken one already by coming in here."

"That's the first I've heard of it!" protested Jakob. "How was I supposed to know that? I'm a stranger here. I haven't spoken to anyone except you. And I was lured in by voices. I wouldn't have entered otherwise."

The head paused. It would not be drawn into an argument. "Some wishes are easily granted," it said at last. "Visions, summoning people . . . these do not alter the fabric of the forest. But some wishes are not so simple. Some wishes bring about change. Yours is such a wish. You would change a fox into a girl. Such wishes must be won. So—let us begin. Choose your sister and I will change her. But beware: you have only one chance."

"*One* chance! You didn't say that yesterday. Did you?"

"I'm saying it now, so listen. *One* chance. Choose wrongly and I cannot help you. Your sister will remain a fox forever."

Jakob turned and gazed at the foxes. They all looked so similar—how could he possibly tell? One was a bit bigger than the others. One was a shade darker. One had a torn ear. One had a blind eye.

But these were tiny differences. And there were so many foxes, he couldn't begin to see those at the back of the crowd.

He started to walk among them. They were all quiet now. Patiently watching. Waiting for him to choose so they could return to their dens. Jakob scanned their faces. Nothing. Then he remembered something.

"My staff! Where is it? Perhaps the globe will glow when I find Mari."

It was lying by the side of the well. The foxes obligingly parted so he could reach it. He started the search again. But the globe didn't glow.

On he went, scanning every face. Holding a picture of Marianna in his mind, hoping it would help. But it didn't.

Or did it? Because just as he was giving up all hope of finding her, he spotted one fox that struck him as different. It wasn't so much the way it *looked* as the way it looked *at him*. It couldn't come forward—it was locked within the crowd—but its gaze suggested it wanted to. It was utterly focused. Intense. Imploring.

And then a strange thing happened. Jakob left his body. The shell was still standing there, holding the staff, surrounded by foxes—but Jakob had become no more than a breath. He felt himself leaving his body through his own nose—*hhhhaaa*—soft as a sigh. Then he picked up speed, flew through the air to the fox's face, and—*hmmm*—the fox breathed him in. Finally he traveled up the long muzzle and found himself looking at the world through the fox's eyes. Everything was brighter. Tighter. He could see the crowd of foxes at eye level. Hear their breathing. Smell their scent.

But more than this, he could feel the emotions of the fox and understand them. In that moment, he knew exactly how it felt to be that fox, standing there in the forest, waiting for something to happen. He *was* that fox. He knew exactly what it was thinking. And it was thinking the same thing, over and over again: *It's me, Jakob! It's me!*

Jakob left Marianna's body, catching a ride on her very next breath. He flew back through the air and into his own body. Felt his fingers curl around the staff once more and—*voomf!*—the globe burst into life, burning with a golden orange glow.

He pushed his way through the foxes till he reached Marianna. He threw his arm around her and held her tight, like he would never let her go. Then he led her back to the well, with the foxes parting before them in great red waves.

And once he was there, he fell to his knees, placed his hand on Marianna's head, and declared, "This is my sister and I wish she was a girl again."

CHAPTER
FORTY-FIVE

The head nodded and the thin lips spoke: "You have chosen well, young hero."

Through the trees came a beam of pure sunlight. It struck the well, gilding the gray eyes, and from them sprang two dazzling rays of golden light that flew like arrows toward Marianna.

As they struck her, she felt herself beginning to change. There was no pain, just a strange woozy sensation, and when she shook her head to clear it, she felt curls brushing her cheek. She was a girl again. She was even wearing the dress she had worn back in Hamelin.

"Mari!" cried Jakob. He threw himself upon her and hugged her again.

"I tried to call out to you," said Marianna breathlessly. "All the time I've been a fox, I've been able to speak, but I couldn't do it then. I don't know why."

"Rules!" laughed Jakob. "I had to win you, Mari, and so I have. Sir Jakob of the New Legs triumphs again!"

Marianna held him at arm's length and looked at him in wonder. "Yes, you *do* have new legs! I couldn't believe it when I saw you walking toward me. How did that happen? And where did you get this amazing staff?"

"I'll tell you later," said Jakob. "I think we need to get out of the forest. We're not supposed to be in here."

Jakob helped Marianna to her feet. It felt strange to her, being upright again, but she knew her body would remember and adjust. She smoothed the creases from her dress while Jakob returned to the well.

"Thank you," he said. "For everything."

The head smiled. "Travel well, my young friend. May your journey be swift and—" It paused and turned in the water, as if sensing something.

"What is it?" asked Jakob quietly.

"Something comes." There was a new expression in the pale gray eyes. Jakob didn't like it.

"Go," said the head urgently. "Go now. And may Fortune watch over you."

Jakob quickly returned to Marianna, took her hand, and led her away.

"What's wrong?" she asked.

"Nothing."

"You're pulling my arm out of its socket! You can't tell me there's nothing wrong! Did the head say something? Jakob?"

"It may be nothing," said Jakob, "but the head thought there was something coming."

"Oh, dear Lord," said Marianna.

Now it was Jakob's turn to feel frightened. The color had drained from Marianna's face.

"What is it, Mari?"

"I don't know for sure," she replied, "but I suspect it's the Piper."

Jakob instantly slowed down. "Well, that's all right! I thought there was some kind of monster coming for us."

"There is," said Marianna. "Please, Jakob—you must come on. There isn't time to explain now. We have to get out of the forest."

"Why?"

"Please, Jakob! Just come!"

Jakob said no more, simply followed his sister through the trees. But Marianna didn't know the way out of the forest and neither did he. Hours went by, they were hopelessly lost, and the light was fading.

Marianna stopped and threw her hands up in despair. "I don't know where we are and it's going to be dark soon."

"I can help with that," said Jakob. His staff began to glow with a warm amber light. He sat down on a nearby stone. "Let's rest awhile, Mari. We've been walking all day."

"There's no time," said Marianna, but she sat

down anyway. And once she was down, her whole body seemed to collapse. Her shoulders slumped and her head hung low.

Jakob thought he had never seen anyone look so broken. "It's all right, Mari," he said. "I'll protect you."

"No," said Marianna. "I'm supposed to protect *you* and I don't think I can. I can't even find a way out of the forest." She closed her eyes—and suddenly pictured her father, back in the lane. She remembered the look on his face as he realized he couldn't hold her. A terrible blend of despair, anger, and fear. And she understood he wasn't being useless. He was doing his best. It wasn't his fault that his best wasn't good enough. Right now, her best wasn't good enough either—and Jakob might die because of it.

"There must be something we can do," said Jakob.

Marianna shook her head. "I can't think of anything."

"Let me try." Jakob closed his eyes and concentrated hard—but nothing happened. "I'm sorry," he said. "I thought maybe I could leave my body and fly up above the trees, but I can't."

Marianna turned. "Why on earth would you think you could do that?"

Jakob shrugged. "I've done it before."

Marianna went cold. This wasn't what she wanted to hear.

"Back at the well," he went on. "I left my body, flew through the air, and went up your nose. I read your thoughts. That's how I knew it was you."

"Have you done any more . . . magic?" said Marianna in a whisper, as if she didn't want the trees to know.

"No. Except for the staff, of course."

"The staff? Are you saying that *you* made it glow just now?"

Jakob grinned. "I think it's this place, Mari. Everyone can do magic here."

Marianna said nothing. She couldn't—her heart was in her mouth. *It was true.* Everything Papa had said was true. Jakob did have magic powers. He *was* the one the Piper was looking for.

She had to get Jakob to safety. Had to protect him, even if it meant risking her own life. But right now the most important thing was to keep calm. If she started to panic, so would Jakob. She didn't want that. They would need to be quick and clearheaded to get out of the forest alive.

"Come on," she said lightly, standing up. "Let's keep walking."

They hurried on, but it wasn't long before Marianna saw what she was dreading: the full moon. A sliver of silver, cutting through the tree canopy. Her heart froze at the sight of it, though she said nothing, just urged her brother on.

Was there no end to the forest? The trees seemed

205

to be gathering together. Huddling close, like chickens when the fox comes. It was so quiet, every footfall thudded into the forest floor. Twigs snapped, leaves rustled, stones rattled. It was impossible to move quickly without making a noise.

And then they heard the howl. A skin-chilling, blood-stilling, hope-killing howl. It flew into the sky. Shattered against the moon. Hammered down like hail. And every creature in the forest—everything that crawled or ran or fluttered or swam—heard the power and the pain behind it.

"Blessed Mary, save us," said Marianna. "It's him."

The howl hadn't ended before another one came, crashing through the night like a bear. Marianna spun around, desperately trying to locate the source. It was outside the forest. No, it was *inside* the forest. Suddenly she wished she were a fox again, with eyes and ears that could tell her exactly when the Beast was coming. A nose that could catch his stench on the wind.

Now she had nothing. Just her wits and her hope and her love for her brother.

"Run, Jakob!" she cried. "Run!"

CHAPTER
FORTY-SIX

Marianna and Jakob ran for their lives, crashing through undergrowth, tearing through brambles. They didn't stop to think where they were going. They ran blindly on, desperately hoping that something would save them. But nothing did.

And soon Marianna caught a familiar smell—the foul stink of the Beast. The hairs rose on the back of her neck. She looked for Jakob. He was right behind her.

"Get in front of me, Jakob!" she shouted, moving to one side. "Where I can see you."

He obeyed and they ran on. But Marianna could hear the Beast now: an extra set of feet pounding the forest floor. Hot and heavy, breaking branches underfoot. It was on all fours, running as a wolf. She heard it panting, quick and excited. Heard the snap of its jaw. Heard the blood pounding in her own veins, coursing through her body like a river in flood, sweeping her along on a tide of terror.

They were twisting and turning now, threading

through the trees, in—out—in—out, fleeing like deer. They burst into a glade and Marianna saw a tree silhouetted in the moonlight: a mighty oak, with a vast, bulbous trunk. And in that moment, she remembered her fox's den—the hollow oak—and prayed that this one had suffered the same fate.

"In there!" she cried. "Into the trunk!" Jakob wriggled into the crack like a caterpillar and she squeezed herself in behind him.

URRAAAAAAH!

Just in time! The Beast slammed against the trunk, setting the whole tree rocking. It raised itself on its rear legs, smacked its front paws down either side of the opening, and thrust its great muzzle inside.

Marianna pushed Jakob back, shielding him with her own body. The stench was unbelievable. Tears sprang to her eyes. She was nearly sick but swallowed it down.

The Beast snapped its jaws. Marianna saw a flash of fangs, and a spray of spittle hit her full in the face. Her eyes closed against it and she kept them closed. She didn't want to see. Hearing was enough. The Beast was tearing strips of bark from the trunk. Scratching and tearing and rending the tree, opening the crack wider and wider.

Suddenly it was done. Marianna opened her eyes just as the great head burst in through the opening, jaws wide, nostrils flaring, lantern eyes fixed on her face. The savage jaws seized hold of her dress and started to pull. Marianna could feel herself sliding through the crack, away from Jakob, into the jaws of the Beast.

"NO!" she wailed. "NO-O-O-O!" But the Beast was too strong. It pulled with the force of a dozen dogs. She couldn't hold on. It dragged her out of the trunk, shook her like a rabbit, then hurled her across the clearing. She fell down and hit her head hard— *duudd*. Darkness descended. She knew no more.

Jakob took his chance. While the Beast was sniffing at Marianna's body, he leaped out of the tree and started to run. He wanted to help Marianna, of course he did, but knew he couldn't. Something inside was urging him to save himself.

But the Beast was behind him. He felt the tremors in the ground as it thundered after him, fangs bared. Felt the thud as it sprang toward him, all four feet leaving the earth. *Doomf!* The Beast hit him with full force in the middle of his back, sending him sprawling to the ground, the breath knocked clean out of his body.

And then he felt his own fingers, fishing for the handle of his sword—the broken bit of branch he had given himself at the start of his quest. And as his fingers curled around it, he closed his eyes and wished it had the power it needed. The power to pierce wolf hide. The power to kill.

Instantly Jakob felt the magic moving within him.

It poured from his heart like molten metal. Ran down his arms. Found his fingers. Entered that twiggy stick and transformed it. The handle became round, smooth, solid. The blade emerged, forged by the heat of his hand. And Jakob, feeling its weight, summoned all his strength, twisted hard, and rolled onto his back. Raised the sword and thrust it into the side of the Beast. Drove it home, then pulled it out again.

Aieee! The howl was so loud, they must have heard it in Hamelin Town. Jakob felt it like a blow to the body. The Beast staggered back, clutching the wound—though more in shock than in pain. It wasn't a killing blow.

Jakob scrambled to his feet and started to run, across the glade, back into the forest. But the Beast was behind him again, wilder than ever. *Ffffoo!* The Beast flew through the air and felled him a second time, then it hauled him to his feet and threw him like a stone.

Jakob soared through the air, his arms and legs flailing. Time seemed to be bending, going so slowly . . . He could see the glade, bathed in moonlight. He could see the Beast glaring at him with murderous eyes. But worse than that, he could see a massive boulder directly underneath him. He couldn't avoid it. It was going to kill him.

Dumm! Unbelievably, Jakob thudded down beside the boulder, bruised but not broken. He stretched out his hand and placed it on the stone. Silently thanked it for not bashing his brains out.

But the Beast was still there. Coming in for the kill now, down on all fours, hackles raised, feet carefully placed, stalking forward, fangs bared, savagely growling, eyes unblinking.

Jakob shrank back against the boulder and prayed for a miracle.

Then he felt something. A tremor, deep within the boulder. A ripple that grew stronger and stronger, till the earth itself seemed to be moving. Jakob fell backward. *The boulder had moved.* And when he turned to see why, he discovered it wasn't a boulder at all.

It was a huge, angry ogre.

CHAPTER
FORTY-SEVEN

Even the Beast stopped advancing when it saw the size of the ogre. The Beast was big, but the ogre was enormous: twice as tall and six times heavier. But it was a creature of very little brain. The eyes that peered out from its craggy face showed neither cunning nor reason. The lumbering body moved in response to the most basic needs and moods: sleep, hunger, thirst, and anger. Unwittingly, Jakob had interrupted one and sparked another. The ogre was tired and angry to be woken.

The ogre sniffed the air and shifted its great bulk. Jakob scuttled away to hide in the bushes, but the ogre had seen him. It began a slow march toward him. *Dum! Dum! Dum! Dum!* The earth shook with each massive footfall. *Dum! Dum! Dum! Dum!* The great gray hands were flexing, the fat fingers wriggling like vipers. *Dum! Dum! Dum! Dum!* Jakob frantically looked for somewhere else to hide. There was a tree he could climb—but the Beast was standing beside it.

The Beast was snarling, shifting, unsure what to do. Like the ogre, it danced to a simple tune. It had just one thought in its head: *Bite the boy*. But it couldn't do it. The ogre was in the way. It had to be stopped.

With a great roar, the Beast sprang through the air and landed on the ogre's back. Its claws dug into the soft flesh of the shoulders. Its fangs seized the fatty neck. Its back feet kicked, viciously shredding the skin like paper.

The ogre bellowed and shook itself, trying to dislodge the Beast. When that didn't work, its mighty hands reached up, grabbed the Beast by its shaggy mane, and pulled. The Beast was thrown completely over the ogre's head. It somersaulted in the air and hit the earth with a sickening thud.

It didn't get up.

With the Beast gone, the ogre turned its attention back to Jakob—who suddenly realized that the ogre couldn't see very well. The creature was sniffing— *hhff-huh-hhff-huh-hhff-huh-hhff*—trying to locate him. And yes, it was huge and heavy and immensely strong, but it was also slow and clumsy. Jakob had quick wits and fast legs—and his staff, if he could remember where he had left it.

Inside the oak!

Jakob sprinted across the glade and reached into the broken oak. He seized the staff, pointed it straight at the lumbering ogre, closed his eyes, and pictured a burst of pure energy. A spear of silver that could fly through the night and pierce the monster's stony heart.

And that is exactly what happened. The staff shuddered in his hand as the energy was released, shooting across the glade like a meteor. Night was banished; the darkness exploded into light as the beam hit its target. And when Jakob opened his eyes, he saw the ogre had gone. Just—*gone*. It had completely disappeared.

Unfortunately, the Beast was still there. It hadn't been killed; it had simply been winded. And as Jakob stepped out from the safety of the tree, it rose unsteadily to its feet.

Jakob saw it coming, but there was nothing he could do. He felt weak and wobbly. All his strength had gone into the staff to deliver the deadly blow. He needed time to recover. Not long—a few minutes—but that was too much to hope for. As soon as the Beast found its bearings, it would attack. Despair fell upon Jakob like a sackful of spiders. Marianna couldn't help him. He couldn't help himself. He was doomed.

And then his father arrived.

CHAPTER
FORTY-EIGHT

Jakob couldn't believe what he was seeing. It had to be a dream, a hallucination, another trick of the forest. But whatever it was, Moller was there. He stumbled out of the trees and paused, swaying on his feet, looking around.

It was such a familiar sight, Jakob thought they could almost be in Hamelin again. One of them drunk and looking for a fight. The other watching, deeply ashamed and desperate.

But Moller wasn't drunk. Not this time. He was exhausted. He had walked all through the night and on through the day, trying to find Marianna. He had had no food and very little water. He had found the forest and been drawn into it. Night had come, he had heard the commotion and followed it. Now he had stumbled into the middle of a nightmare. The Beast was alive but Marianna was dead and Jakob was about to join her.

The Beast began to run, bounding across the glade toward Jakob. Moller saw it coming and felt fury rise within him. He hurled himself between the Beast and his boy: "NO-O-O-O-O!"

But the cry was ripped from his body. The Beast swiped Moller with a killing paw and he was cut like a peach. A five-claw wound, deep and deadly, from chest to belly.

"NO-O-O-O-O!" echoed Jakob. He saw Moller fall to the floor, spinning like a wind-torn leaf. Saw the Beast hurtling toward him again. His fingers curled tighter around his staff. He pointed it at the Beast, knowing it wouldn't save him—*couldn't* save him—but it might do something.

And it *did* do something. The globe started to glow and an enormous bubble appeared around him—a shining, iridescent sphere, just like the ones the Piper had made in Hamelin. Jakob knew it wouldn't last long. He didn't have the strength to hold it forever. But while it lasted, the Beast couldn't harm him.

The Beast skidded to a halt and stared at Jakob through the shimmer of the sphere. Jakob could feel the heat from its breath. Smell the blood on its tongue. See the madness in its eyes. But there was something else too. Something lurking *behind* the eyes. A spirit, a force, a will that wasn't entirely bestial.

Jakob was intrigued. What was it? He had to know.

He closed his eyes and concentrated, and soon

he was leaving his body. Through the sphere he went, like a berry seed blown on the wind. Into a nostril . . . up the nose . . . into the skull . . . into the mind of the Beast.

Jakob looked out through the Beast's eyes and saw himself, protected by the bubble. He could feel the Beast's emotions: frustration, anger, confusion. There was patience too. Pure animal patience—a willingness to wait until the magic disappeared.

But Jakob sensed something more. Somewhere inside this hunter's mind—trapped, hidden, held hostage—there was a light. It was dim, no brighter than the flame on a dying candle, but it was there. *The Piper.*

Jakob traveled through the Beast's body, down to its hot, beating heart. There he found the light and entered it. Oh! It was like falling into a bottomless pool. He was overwhelmed by emotions, thoughts, and memories. He was swimming through hopes and desires. He could see everything. Understand everything.

He knew how it felt to be the Beast, hunting and killing, gorging on blood and still wanting more. He knew how it felt to be the Piper, enduring the shame and self-loathing.

He felt the burden of the curse. Saw the rise and fall of hope over the centuries. A rumor of rats and it grew like corn—and ripened to gold—only to be cut down in another bleak harvest.

And Jakob learned where he fitted in this messy, sorry saga. He knew why the Piper had come to Hamelin Town. What he had been looking for. What he needed.

It was time to leave. Jakob had had enough of this broken battleground of a body, with its dark dungeon of a heart. So he left the Beast, floated through the sphere, and safely returned to his own body. And when his fingers regripped the staff, he made a discovery. While he had been away, his power had renewed itself, many times over. He was saved. He had more than enough power to kill the Beast.

Jakob took a deep breath and readied himself. He moved the staff till it was pointing directly at the Beast's heart. He closed his eyes—and knew he couldn't do it.

The Beast wasn't evil. The Piper wasn't evil. They were just trapped inside bodies they didn't want. Jakob could understand that. He would remember his twisted legs and curved back till the day he died. But he would also remember how it felt to get a new body. He had felt free. Weightless. Incredibly happy.

He wasn't happy now. Marianna was dead. His father was dead. He had nothing left to live for. So why was he about to kill the Beast? Why take a life to save his own when he didn't really want it? It made no sense. It would be better to give his life to someone who *did* want it. Someone who needed it. Someone who had waited centuries to have it.

Jakob looked into the eyes of the Beast and nodded. Drew himself up to his full height. Closed his eyes—and burst the protective bubble.

CHAPTER
FORTY-NINE

Marianna opened her eyes and saw nothing but stars. She frowned and a jagged pain stabbed her between the eyes. *Stars? Ah, it's the sky*, she thought. *I'm lying on my back. Why am I . . . oh! Jakob!*

She sat up. The glade was bathed in moonlight. There was the oak. And there was the Beast. He was—

"NO-O-O-O-O-O!"

The Beast dropped Jakob at the sound of her cry, but she was too late. The Beast had already bitten him.

Marianna stumbled toward them, wondering why the Beast didn't run away. It just stood there, swaying on its feet, its mouth wet with blood. Then its legs buckled and it collapsed, hitting the ground with a terrible *thump*.

But Marianna paid the Beast no attention. She fell to her knees and cradled Jakob in her arms. Rocked him back and forth like he was a baby again.

"Jakob!" she moaned. "Jakob!"

"Is that you, Mari?"

"Jakob?" Marianna couldn't believe it. Her brother's eyes were opening.

He smiled faintly. "I thought . . . you were dead, Mari."

"No," said Marianna. "Just knocked out cold. But you . . ." She couldn't bear to go on.

Jakob reached for her arm and patted it reassuringly. "I . . . don't think I'm . . . dying," he said. "I think I'll be . . . better soon." He opened his eyes wider and managed to focus on her face. Then he remembered. "Papa! You must help him, Mari."

"Papa? Is he here?"

Jakob nodded. "Over there."

Marianna laid Jakob carefully down and looked around. She saw a body. "Papa?" She stumbled toward it. "*Papa!*"

Moller was wet with blood. He was so badly hurt, Marianna didn't dare move him. She knelt and eased his shirt open. The wound was appalling. Five long scratches, desperately deep. Marianna turned her face away and put her hand on his forehead. She stroked the damp hair away from his face. He looked old. So old. Tears pricked her eyes.

"Mari?" Moller's eyelids flickered open. "Mari, I've found you."

"Yes, Papa. I'm here."

"Take my hand, Mari."

Marianna took it and held it tight.

"Did I save him, Mari? I tried."

"Yes, Papa," said Marianna. "You saved him. He's going to be fine."

Moller squeezed her hand. "I'm glad." He looked at Marianna and managed to smile. But she saw the light fading from his eyes.

"Don't leave me," she whispered.

"I'll never leave you," said Moller. "You're my little girl, Mari." He closed his eyes.

"Papa?"

Moller was struggling to breathe. Marianna saw him gather himself for one last try.

"Papa?"

But he simply sighed . . . and was gone.

Marianna felt his hand go limp. "No," she whimpered. "No. Papa? Papa!"

There was no reply. Marianna stared at him in horror. She shook her head and gulped for air. Then the tears came. Great racking sobs that shook her whole body.

The tears rolled down her cheeks and down her nose. Down her chin and onto the dead body of her father. *Drip-drip-drip* onto the wound.

The wound began to heal.

Marianna didn't notice at first. She was still lost in grief. But in between sobs, she happened to glance down.

"Dear heaven!"

The flesh was pulling itself together. Soon the gashes had disappeared, leaving nothing but silver scars, slender as threads. Then Moller's mouth opened and the air rushed in. His body rose up. He was bending like a bridge. Marianna fell back, terrified. But there was nothing to fear. Life had been rekindled in her father. His chest began to rise and fall as he breathed again.

Marianna crept closer. "Papa?"

Moller opened his eyes, closed them with a sigh, stretched lazily, then opened them again.

"Papa? Is that you?"

"Of course it's me, Mari. Who else would it be?" He sat up slowly. "What happened? I feel like I've been kicked all over. And why am I covered in blood?"

Marianna stared at him in amazement. "Don't you remember?"

Moller stared right back at her. He shook his head. Then he put his hand on his chest, frowned . . . gasped . . . and remembered everything. The color slid from his face.

"Is Jakob all right?" he asked.

"Yes," said Marianna. "Though I think he could use a bit of magic too. He's over there." She helped her father to his feet and together they walked across the glade.

Jakob had managed to move himself. He was lying with his back propped up against the oak. Beside him lay the Piper, fast asleep and quite naked.

Marianna blushed when she saw him. "We can't leave him like that," she said. "It's not decent. We'll have to do something."

Jakob nodded weakly. "He also has a wound that needs tending. I stabbed him with my sword."

"That twiggy old stick?"

Jakob smiled. "The finest sword a boy ever had." He closed his eyes and breathed deeply. "Fetch me some leaves, Mari. The biggest you can find."

She hurried off and returned with six enormous leaves, each one big enough to wrap a baby. Jakob pointed his staff at them, closed his eyes and—*voomf!*—instantly they were changed into clothes. Marianna dropped them like they were snakes.

Jakob laughed. "What's the matter?"

"It's this magic business," said Marianna. She picked them up and placed them beside the Piper. "I don't think I'll ever get used to it!"

CHAPTER
FIFTY

Marianna and Jakob withdrew to the far side of the glade while their father tended to the Piper's wound. Once that was done, Moller joined them and they started to exchange stories. Soon an hour had gone by, and still they were lost in a world of foxes, elves, Standing Stones, and ancient wells. Moller listened intently, especially when Jakob talked about his surprising new talent for magic.

"Your mother suspected it, you know," he said. "The moment you were born, Jakob, she held you in her arms and said, *He's special, this one.* And I know she worried that one day someone from Elvendale might find you. Not the Piper—someone from her own family, come to claim you as their own. She wanted me to protect you." He sighed deeply. "I haven't done a good job."

Marianna briefly put her hand on his. "You've tried," she said quietly.

Moller glanced at her in surprise. She flushed slightly but said no more. Moller felt his heart move, hardened though it was by life's sorrows. He lowered his head and smiled.

Jakob hadn't noticed the exchange. He was too busy thinking about magic. "You're special too, though, Mari, aren't you? You brought Papa back to life."

"I didn't," said Marianna, startled.

"You did! You cried, didn't you? It was the tears. They healed the wound."

"No," said Marianna. She shook her head, not wanting it to be true. "It wasn't me. Mama never said I was special, did she, Papa? No, I thought not. It wasn't me, Jakob. It must have been the forest, working some kind of magic."

Jakob looked at her curiously. "I don't know why you're getting upset, Mari. I think it's great to have magic powers! And I still believe it was you."

"No," said Marianna hotly. "It wasn't. I'm not special. If I am—how do you explain the Standing Stone? I told you, the Piper made me touch it. It didn't respond."

"Actually, it did."

The Piper was standing beside them, fully clothed and smiling.

"What?"

"It did respond," said Finn. "But it was so faint, I knew you weren't the one I was looking for. Believe me, if Jakob had touched it, the whole of Elvendale would have known about it."

He smiled again—the warm, easy smile they all remembered from Hamelin. But then he turned serious and, to Marianna's amazement, he dropped to one knee before Jakob.

"Thank you," he said. "A thousand times, thank you. You cannot begin to imagine the joy I feel in my heart today."

Jakob smiled. "I wanted to help."

"And you have," said Finn. "Though at great cost to yourself."

Jakob simply shrugged, but Marianna pounced.

"What do you mean—*at great cost*?"

When Finn didn't reply, Marianna pushed him—so hard, he nearly fell over. "What do you mean?"

"I was cursed," he said. "To be the Beast, every full moon. There was only one cure. To pass it to another."

Marianna stared at him. "Are you saying that . . . *Jakob* is cursed now? That he'll become a beast every full moon?"

Finn nodded.

Marianna threw herself at him, nails aimed at his face. Finn caught her by the wrists and held her. She fought him like a baited badger.

"*Whoa* there!" cried Moller, trying unsuccessfully to pull her off.

"Let him be, Mari!" cried Jakob, joining in the fray. "Let him be."

But Marianna fought on. "You've ruined his life,"

she screamed at Finn. "You have condemned my brother to endless torment. Years of suffering."

"He knew," said Finn.

Marianna didn't hear him.

"HE KNEW."

Marianna stopped struggling. "What?"

"Jakob knew what would happen," said Finn. "He allowed me to do it."

Marianna went limp in his hands. Finn put her down, grimacing in pain from the wound in his side.

"Is this true?" said Marianna, turning to Jakob. "You *let* him do it?"

Jakob nodded.

"Why?"

"I understood him," said Jakob. "I shared his thoughts—his feelings—just for a moment. I saw what he wanted to do—and what it would mean for me. But I also saw *why* he needed to do it, and I wanted to help. So I didn't fight. I let him bite me."

Moller whistled. "That was brave, boy."

Jakob shrugged. "Not really."

"He could have killed you," said Marianna. "He killed Papa."

"'I humbly apologize for that," interrupted Finn. "That was the Beast. It was uncontrollable."

"I know," said Marianna angrily. "I saw what it did to Karl. And now we have a new beast. My brother."

"Mari," said Moller. "Let's not go around in circles. Piper—tell me the truth now. None of your tricks. Will my boy become a beast, next full moon?"

Finn slowly shook his head. "I cannot say—and that is an honest answer. I know that I am free of the Beast. I can feel it in my heart, in my head, in my bones. It has truly gone. Jakob—can you feel it? A shadow at the back of your mind? A feeling that you are not entirely alone?"

Jakob fell silent, concentrating. "I don't know," he said at last.

Marianna felt the tears spring to her eyes. Moller rose to his feet and started to walk away, as if he would find answers elsewhere. But then he turned back.

"What's to be done?" he said. "Is there no cure?"

"I fear not," said Finn. "Unless . . ."

". . . he passes it on," finished Marianna. "Then he will *never* be cured. Never. Because Jakob won't do that."

Finn glanced at Jakob's face and knew it to be true. "We must have hope," he said. "I was cursed because I did wrong, I admit that. But Jakob has done nothing wrong. Perhaps the curse has died tonight."

"I pray so," said Moller. "Only time will tell. But what's to become of us now? Do you know a way out of this forest?"

"No," said Finn, "but my hawk will find us in the morning. He will lead us out."

"And what then?" said Marianna to her father. "Shall we leave Elvendale?"

"I reckon so," said Moller. "Perhaps the Piper here will find us a door?"

"Gladly," said Finn. "You shall have a door to wherever you want."

"To Hamelin, of course," said Marianna. "Home." Her thoughts immediately flew back to town. Back to the narrow streets and the bustling market square, back to her friends and the gossip she was missing. But then she realized—her friends weren't there. Her friends were in Elvendale. They were bats and badgers and whatever else the Piper had condemned them to be.

Later, as she made a bed of leaves, she glanced across at Finn. What a strange creature he was. So fickle! It was as if all the extremes of being were there, wrapped up in one beautiful, tormented body. And he *was* beautiful. Even now, after everything he had done—to Jakob, to her friends, to her—she couldn't deny it. But then, the deadly nightshade plant was beautiful too, with its bell-like flowers and shiny black berries. Dark, *poisonous* berries that brought death to all who ate them.

Ratcatcher, Piper, enchanter, elf . . . Whoever he was, whatever he was, Marianna wished, with all her heart, that he had never darkened the gates of Hamelin Town.

CHAPTER
FIFTY-ONE

Morning came, bringing Flyte with it. He descended from the clouds with a silver pipe held firmly in his talons, dropped it into Finn's eager hands, then landed on his outstretched arm.

"We need you to lead us out of here," said Finn, tucking the pipe in a pocket. "Is it far to the forest edge?"

"Far enough when you're an unwelcome visitor," said Flyte. "You should leave without delay. There's a path south of here. Follow me. I'll take you to it."

With that, Flyte flew across the glade, landed on a tree, and waited for the travelers to join him. Once they did, he flew to another and then another, leading them toward the path and safety.

They made good progress. The path, when they reached it, was wide and straight. The day was pleasantly warm rather than hot, and there were plenty of pools to drink from. Marianna wished they were carrying a picnic: there were so many inviting places to stop and rest. And there were *endless* things to look at. She longed to linger. They were going home; soon she would have nothing but memories of Elvendale. She wanted to make sure they were vivid ones.

But the Piper was setting a punishing pace, despite his wound. He marched on, not stopping for anything. Whenever the hawk came close, he asked the same question: how far? And every time he heard the answer, he frowned and pushed on.

Then they came to a blissful place. The air was sweet with scent. The path was lined with flowers of every color and hue, like crowds waiting for a procession. Above the flowers danced butterflies. Clouds of them; swirls of them. Peacock blue and jasper green; purple with a satin sheen; pancake yellow, midnight ink; sugar white and blushing pink. Marianna was entranced. She paused to watch a beautiful blue one as it unrolled its long tongue down into a golden flower funnel. It drank the sweet nectar and Marianna sighed. She longed to taste it too.

"Marianna! You are lingering!"

Finn had grabbed her roughly by the elbow.

"Yes, I am," she said, shaking him off. "And why shouldn't I? I want to remember these lovely things. I won't be returning to this forest ever again."

"Nor I," said Finn darkly. "Please, we must leave here." He glanced over his shoulder and then walked on, trusting her to follow.

"You're scared," said Marianna, catching up to

him. "*Really* scared, aren't you? Why? Does something live in this forest?"

"I do not know," said Finn. "But I do know this: we are not welcome here. Entering the forest is forbidden, and I have done so twice. My presence here will not have gone unnoticed."

"You think we're being watched?" whispered Marianna.

"I know so. Watched and followed. Can you not feel it?"

Marianna shook her head. Suddenly the day had lost its sparkle. She hurried on, aware now that the forest showed no sign of ending. All around, the trees seemed trapped—held in a perpetual world of shadows, waiting for something for happen.

Then she saw a light moving behind the trees. A strange, unearthly glow that grew brighter as it approached. It leaped onto the path, blocking their way, and the light was so unbearably bright, Marianna had to shield her eyes. But then it faded and she saw a stag. A ghostly silver stag, with magnificent antlers and an ethereal light playing about its body.

The stag stared at Finn with milky eyes. "You have returned."

"I had no choice," said Finn, stepping forward. "I have no desire to be here."

"Yet you *are* here," said the stag, with a stamp of a shiny hoof. "And you are cured."

Finn nodded. "I am. But I have suffered."

"That is true," said the stag, "and I am content. I have had my revenge. But my master would have you suffer more."

Finn frowned. "Your master? Who is he?'"

The stag made no reply.

"Why would he have me suffer more? I carried your curse for two hundred and fifty years. Is that not suffering enough?"

"Time means little to my master," said the stag. "He is so very old."

"I have repented," said Finn. "Not a day has gone by without my reproaching myself. But let me say it again—here, before you, before witnesses—I am truly sorry for entering the forest that day and hunting you down."

"My master knows that. And he agrees: you have paid the price for your folly. But that was then. This is now. And you are here, in the forest, for a second time. You are not welcome, Finn. My master is angry."

"Then let him show himself!" cried Finn hotly. "I grow tired of these games. You play with me like a cat plays with a mouse. Where is he? Let him show himself!"

"He is here," said the stag, "all around you, in everything you see. He is the forest, Finn, and you will pay for trespassing."

And with that, the stag lowered its mighty antlers and charged straight at him.

CHAPTER
FIFTY-TWO

Whooo! The ghostly stag passed right through Finn's body. Finn staggered backward, buffeted by the wind of its passing. But he was unharmed. He watched the stag disappear into the heart of the forest.

"Is it over?" said Jakob. "Have you paid the price?"

Finn shook his head. "I fear not. We must hurry on. Ah! Flyte!"

The hawk descended.

"How far, Flyte?"

"An hour's walking and you'll be out," said the hawk. "But there's something in the air; I can feel it. A call. A gathering. I can't say any more than that."

He returned to the sky and Finn started off down the path. The others followed, their faces pale as pastry. Finn's fear was wildly infectious.

Moller caught up with Finn and kept pace. "Will you be able to protect us if anything attacks?" he asked.

"No," replied Finn. "Magic only happens in here if the forest allows it." He pulled his pipe from his pocket, put it to his lips and blew. No sound came. "You see? Useless."

"What's that noise?"

Marianna had stopped dead in her tracks. "Can you hear it?"

The others froze and listened. They could hear it too: a low, insistent drone, coming closer, getting louder.

In a flash of golden feathers, Flyte dropped from the sky.

"SNAPPERBUGS!" he cried. "RUN FOR COVER!"

An enormous black cloud was whizzing down the path toward them. Within seconds, it was directly overhead: a dark, deadly battalion of beetles. Fat black beetles, big as fists, armed with pincers and snapping mandibles. Then the attack began.

Vumm! Vumm-vumm! They fell like stones, viciously nipping and biting as they found flesh. When the travelers knocked them off, they tumbled to the ground and lay on their backs, angrily kicking their legs till they righted themselves. Then they spread their wings, flew back into the cloud, and attacked again.

Marianna fled to the cover of the trees. She hated bugs and beetles, and these were monstrous things. But Jakob and Moller stood firm and tried to help

Finn. They were all getting bitten, but clearly he was the main target. Wherever he went the cloud followed, even when he dived under the trees. Now he was running up and down the path, howling in pain, while Moller tried to bat the snapperbugs away with a stick.

Thood! Moller hit them full force, but the snapperbugs didn't squish. They were too well armored. They simply sailed through the air, fell to the ground, and picked themselves up.

Stupid creatures, thought Marianna. *Why don't they open their wings before they hit the ground? EOW!* Moller was batting them in her direction! A fat beetle fell in her lap and lay there wriggling. It was enormous—all feet and feelers. She leaped up and ran back to the path.

Jakob saw her coming. "Marianna! Do something!" He was holding his staff high, willing it to work, but it wouldn't.

Marianna did the only thing she could think of. She stamped on the nearest snapperbug as it fell to the ground. She twisted her boot, grinding it hard against the earth. There was a sharp crack as the beetle's armor shattered. She whooped and looked for more.

But suddenly the attack was over. The snapperbugs rose into the air as if they had been summoned and sped off, the great cloud weaving through the trees like smoke.

Finn sank to his knees. His whole body was quivering; his eyes were glazed like pools in winter. His neck and hands were bloody with bites. His face was purple and swollen, like an overripe plum.

"Come on," said Moller, hauling him to his feet. "We're going."

"I cannot," said Finn. "I do not have the strength."

"Then find it! You can't stay here and we're not leaving you."

"You should save yourselves," said Finn. "The forest won't let me leave."

"We'll see about that," said Moller. "Jakob! Take the other side, that's a good lad."

With the Piper supported, they moved off down the path.

"Do you think that's it, Papa?"

Jakob had whispered, but there was no need. The Piper was beyond listening.

"I'd like to think so," said Moller. "But there's an old saying: Bad things come in threes. I fear that was just the beginning."

CHAPTER
FIFTY-THREE

The travelers journeyed on. Marianna walked ahead of the others, proudly bearing Jakob's staff. She was acting as the eyes and ears of the party, and she was taking the role seriously. If there was danger ahead, their lives might depend upon her seeing it. So far, she had seen nothing alarming. But now she noticed the forest was changing. The broad-leaved oaks and elegant alders were thinning. Ahead lay pines—thousands of them—tall, slender, and silent. It was so dark between them, it could almost be evening.

Marianna paused and scanned the new land-scape. She tilted her head like a fox and smiled as she caught herself doing it. She wished her old supersenses remained. She could certainly use them now. As it was, she just had to hope for the best.

She led them on. It was so quiet. No birds or insects. No sounds at all. Just the pad of their boots against the needled floor and the occasional grunt from Finn.

Five minutes passed. Six, seven, eight . . . Nothing had happened. But then Marianna felt the hairs starting to rise on her arms and on the back of her neck. Her breath was shortening. Her eyes were widening, all on their own. Something was shifting in the forest, getting ready to attack.

The trees! They didn't move, didn't bend, didn't make a sound. They just fired.

Zzoooo! Zzoo-zzoo! Millions of pine needles flew through the air.

Zzooo! Zzooo! Zzoo-zzoo-zzoo! Razor sharp and deadly. So many, they couldn't fail to hit.

Aiee! The needles hit hard and dug in deep like bee stings. Jakob and Moller turned in on Finn, shielding him with their bodies, so most of their needles struck their jackets and fell to the floor. But Marianna wasn't so lucky. She howled and ran, as fast as she could, desperately trying to reach safety, while the needles whistled and whizzed around her. She flailed her arms, swinging them around like windmill sails, but it didn't help. It was like running through a cloud of mosquitoes. She could bat hundreds away, but the few that made it through caused terrible pain.

But she could see safety. Ahead lay a tangled, green wildwood. Sycamores and blackthorn; beeches and brambles. With a sob of relief, she burst out of the nightmarish pines into the warm embrace of the broad leaves.

Marianna threw herself down on a grassy bank, closed her eyes, and felt the *thud* as the others joined her. She sat up. Moller, Jakob, and the Piper were such a tangle of legs and arms, she couldn't see where one ended and the next began. All of them were prickly as hedgehogs. Finn was barely conscious.

"*Owww!*" said Jakob, untangling himself. "*Owww! I* don't understand. Why did the pines shoot at us as well as Finn?"

"We're helping him escape," said Moller. "The forest hates us all now."

"Then it's a mean, vicious beast," said Jakob angrily, wincing as he pulled out needle after needle. "It doesn't understand friendship."

He turned to Finn and started pulling needles out of the Piper's face. "I don't care what it sends next—I won't leave you. DO YOU HEAR THAT, FOREST? I WON'T LEAVE HIM. I mean it, Mari. I didn't save Finn to lose him to the forest. If it wants him, it'll have to fight me first."

Above their heads, the leaves rustled, as if a message was passing through the trees.

"Listen," said Marianna. "The trees are talking to one another."

"Good," said Jakob. "That means they heard me."

Marianna couldn't help smiling. Jakob was so fierce! She wished the people of Hamelin could see him like this. "Crooked Jakob"—that's what they called him. *Ha!* They would see him differently now! They would see he was strong and brave and spirited. Exactly the kind of person you would want by your side when life became difficult.

But the strange thing was, Jakob had always been like that. It had nothing to do with the magic of Elvendale. He had been a hero even as he clumped around town on his crutch. It hadn't been easy for him, Marianna knew. The teasing had hurt. He would hold back the tears until he reached home, but Marianna had seen them. She had watched him struggle to do chores too. Sometimes he returned from the water pump with barely any water in the bucket—the rest had been spilled in the lane. But he insisted on doing his bit to help her.

Sometimes his legs had ached. She had rubbed liniment on them and told him he would feel better in the morning. Did he? Maybe not, but it never stopped him. Day after day, year after year, he had thrown himself onto the tide of humanity that flowed through the streets of Hamelin Town. He had never complained, even through the bad times.

Now Jakob had fetched water from a nearby stream. He was wiping the Piper's face, trying to revive him. *He has such a big heart*, thought Marianna. *I wouldn't do that!* But then, her memories of Finn were different. Jakob hadn't known that bleak, desperate moment in the caves when Finn announced they wouldn't be going home. Hadn't seen him casually throw children into the terrifying eat-or-be-eaten world of animals. Hadn't seen the horror of what he did to Karl. And yes, Finn had his reasons—Marianna knew that now—but still she couldn't forgive him. Would Jakob, if he were she?

Yes, she thought. *He probably would! With his big heart, how could he do otherwise?*

CHAPTER
FIFTY-FOUR

The fresh water seemed to do the trick. Finn opened his eyes and studied Jakob's face.

"Are we out?" he said at last.

"Nearly," said Jakob. "Not far now."

Finn closed his eyes and winced. Jakob couldn't begin to imagine the pain the Piper was in. The pine needles had been bad enough, but Finn had snapperbug bites too. Dozens of them. And even worse, he had the stab wound. No wonder he was weak! Blood was seeping through his shirt and Jakob felt guilty just looking at it. He desperately wanted to repair the damage he had done but he couldn't. Not yet. Magic would work in the forest only if the forest allowed it, and whatever was out there seemed to be enjoying Finn's pain.

They had been rough with him too, Jakob and Moller, dragging him along the path to escape from the pines. Finn should be rolling in agony; Jakob was amazed he wasn't. And very impressed. This was courage.

"I've spoken to the hawk," said Moller, coming over. "He says there's a hill ahead—not very steep— and once we're down the other side, we're out." He helped Finn to his feet. "Can you walk?"

Finn nodded. "I believe I can. I am certainly willing to try."

On they went. Soon they saw the hill. It was curiously narrow—no wider than four men lying head to toe—and it rose no higher than the tallest trees.

"That's hardly a hill at all!" said Marianna. "We'll be over it in no time."

"It's a bit strange," said Moller cautiously. "There are no trees growing on it. Perhaps we should go around."

"We can't," said Jakob. "The trees are packed tight on either side, see? We'd have to fight our way through."

Finn said nothing. He had a bad feeling about the hill but hoped he was wrong.

They walked on. The path grew dusty beneath their feet. As they reached the crown of the hill, they all felt a *thud*, down in the earth below. Then another, and another.

"Do you have dwarves in Elvendale?" Moller asked Finn.

A look of bewilderment passed over Finn's face.

"Dwarves work underground, don't they?" Moller reasoned. "Digging for gold and what have you."

Finn shook his head. "I don't think it is dwarves.

Their mines are in the mountains—and the beat is too regular for pickaxes."

"Maybe it's moles!" said Jakob. "Huge moles, big as bears, with feet like snow shovels!"

Marianna pushed him playfully and they walked on, over the brow of the hill.

"There it is!" cried Jakob. "The end of the forest!"

And so it was. Beyond lay the soft, felted fields of Elvendale, with the high peak of Hamelin Hill basking in the distance. The travelers thought they had never seen anything so beautiful.

They started to descend. But the ground began to move beneath them, as if something was stirring, awakening. The angle of the hill sharpened dramatically, throwing them all off balance. Soon they were tumbling, head over heels, down the hill. Only it wasn't a hill any more. It was a worm. A monstrous white worm, rising up out of the earth where it had slumbered for centuries. As the travelers hit the ground, its eyeless head rose above them like an enormous serpent. The great mouth opened and out shot a tongue, red and forked, as long as a lane.

Marianna flattened herself against the ground. Finn managed to roll out of reach. But Jakob and Moller had fallen on their backs, helpless as beetles. The mighty tongue caught them both and—*THLP!*—they disappeared into the mouth of the worm.

CHAPTER
FIFTY-FIVE

Jakob and Moller were thrown into darkness. They could feel the monster's mouth: wet and warm and cavernous. Jakob reached out a hand and felt a fang. It was huge and smooth, like one of the stalactites in Hamelin Hill.

Then the worm swallowed and they were tumbling through tunnels, miles and miles of them. Whooshing along through the darkness, being bumped and banged at every turn—till they landed with a *thud* in the creature's long-empty stomach.

It was dark. So dark. Jakob wished he had his staff with him, but it had been left outside.

"Papa?" he said. "Are you there?"

"Aye," said his father. "I am, and no bones broken."

"What'll we do, Papa? How will we get out?"

It was a small voice, brave but fearful, like the call of a lost lamb. And there, in the dark, Moller suddenly felt scared to be a father. It was such an overwhelming responsibility. Jakob needed him. He was asking for help. Looking for answers. Wanting reassurance. Trusting that all these things would come from him—Moller—his useless, good-for-nothing wastrel of a father.

Poor little lad. He was going to be disappointed again. It broke Moller's heart to admit it, but it was true. And with that thought, tears came to his eyes, grown man that he was. He was glad it was dark; at least Jakob didn't have to see him crying.

"Papa? What'll we do?"

The voice again, a little more anxious now. Moller felt he was being torn apart, shredded by the stomach of the worm. But it wasn't the worm—the huge, mighty worm—that was tearing at his heart. It was a nine-year-old boy who couldn't begin to understand what he was doing.

Moller heard a shuffling sound. Jakob was coming toward him on all fours, feeling his way forward. And when Jakob found him, he wrapped his arms around his father and curled up close.

Moller felt the breath catching in his chest. Jakob hadn't done that since he was a little lad. *Papa's little dormouse*—that's what his mother had called him. Jakob always wanted to curl up on Moller's lap when he was tiny. It was a bit of a struggle. There would be an elbow sticking out here and a crooked leg there. But they always managed, Jakob and him.

Moller reached down, put his arm around Jakob, and pulled him closer still. He could feel his son's heart, beating in the dark, strong and true. That's what Jakob needed him to be, wasn't it? Strong and true. Well, he couldn't promise it, but he would do his best. He could do no more.

Moller took a deep breath, sighed it away, and wiped his face with his sleeve.

"Son," he said, "this is what we're going to do. We're going to fight this monster and win."

"How?" asked Jakob. "We don't have any weapons."

"We have this."

Moller fished something out of his pocket and placed it in his son's hands. Jakob felt something square and polished.

"It's your tinderbox! Are we going to start a fire?"

"We are," said Moller. "But first we've got to find something—the liver!"

And so they went in search of the worm's liver. Round and round they tramped, exploring the tunnels. The search became easier the farther they traveled, because the insides of the worm began to glow with a strange green light. And soon they found it. An immense brown mass, spongy to the touch and warm with blood.

Moller pulled out a pocketknife and hacked a hole in the liver. Then he took off his jacket, stuffed it into the hole, and began to strike the flint from his tinderbox. A spark landed on the cloth; the cloth

249

started to smolder; the smolder became a burn; the burn became a blaze. The cavernous gut began to fill with smoke.

"We're done," said Moller. "Let's get going!"

They started to run. Down the tunnels, back through the stomach, up toward the throat. The worm was wriggling around them, sending great, muscular spasms rippling along the meaty walls. The smoke was rising. Soon the monster would cough.

The worm began to raise its head. Jakob and Moller slid backward, desperately trying to catch a hold on the slippery insides. Down they went, tumbling back toward the belly, when suddenly: *KKKKKRRRR!* The worm gave an almighty cough, the jaws opened wide, and Jakob and Moller were spat out like cherry stones. They shot through the air and landed in a heap. Marianna rushed over and helped Jakob to his feet.

"You did it!" she said. "I knew you would. Finn said you'd be stuck in there forever, but I said, *No! Jakob will find a way out!*"

"It wasn't me, Mari," said Jakob. "It was Papa. I was completely stumped—just sitting there in the dark, thinking we were doomed. But Papa was brilliant. He came up with a perfect plan. And here we are!"

Marianna looked at her father, openly amazed. Moller was glowing like a pumpkin lantern—

though he tried to shrug it off, as if defeating monsters was something he did most days.

But there wasn't time to stand around feeling proud. Behind them, the worm was hissing furiously.

"RUN!" shouted Moller. "SHE'S GOING TO BLOW!"

Inside the worm, the liver was blazing like a bonfire. The worm started to twist and turn, coiling itself in endless circles. The head turned this way and that, blindly scanning the forest, as if searching for something. What? No one knew. If it was hoping for help, none came. The fearsome tongue flicked. Licked the air, looking for water. But it was too late. The worm raised its head to the sky and a spear of flame burst from its throat. Up into the sky it went, a fountain of fire to rival the sun, and the body of the worm was burned in an instant. Fat flakes fell from the sky, hot and greasy, black as burned pancakes. They peppered the trees. Littered the ground. Crumbled underfoot as the travelers ran away from the mess, away from the forest and anything else it cared to throw at them.

PART
SIX

CHAPTER
FIFTY-SIX

"So," said the Piper, "where do you choose? Hamelin?"

They were standing deep inside Hamelin Hill at a junction of tunnels. Finn was holding his pipe high, filling the cavern with a soft golden glow. Ahead lay four stone arches, each with a tunnel beyond.

"Of course, Hamelin," said Marianna.

"Are you sure about that?"

Oooh! Marianna wanted to slap him. Why was he wasting their time like this? Where else would they be going? Hamelin was their home. The sooner they were there, the sooner life could return to normal. Yes, it had been an extraordinary adventure and she would remember it forever, but now she was tired. She longed for the warmth and safety of her own bed.

But when she looked at the others, she realized why Finn was asking. Her father looked distinctly uncomfortable, while Jakob was pale and anxious.

"What's the matter?" she said.

255

"I don't think we can return to Hamelin," said Moller evenly. He didn't want to upset Marianna. Not here, not now.

Marianna stared at him, slack jawed. "Why ever not?"

"Just think for a moment, Mari. If we go back to town now, how will we explain things? Everyone knows you went with the Piper. If they see you, there'll be a stampede. The whole town will run to Hamelin Hill, expecting to find their children. And they won't, will they? We'll raise their hopes, only to crush them again. That would be cruel, Mari. We can't do it."

"We can make up a story," said Marianna. "We can say I didn't go with the Piper. You found me wandering on the hillside—alone."

"So why didn't Jakob find you? He went up there every day for a week—people know that. Why didn't he see you? And how do we explain Jakob? Say he was healed by sitting on a hillside? I don't think so."

"There must be something we can do," said Marianna wearily.

"If there is, I can't see it," said Moller. "I've been worrying about this for hours, Mari, turning it over and over in my mind. We can't tell them the truth, so we'll have to lie. Spin some elaborate tale and hope to God they believe it. Because they might not. You know what some of them are like. The miller, for one. Can you imagine him, Mari? He'll take one look at our Jakob and within a week he'll be muttering, 'Witchcraft.' Stirring up trouble, like he always does. I don't want that for the lad. He's had it hard enough these past few years."

Marianna looked at Jakob. Her father was right. Jakob couldn't take any more abuse from the town. But there had to be some solution.

"I have it!" she cried. "They won't care about Jakob if the children return! Finn, you can play your pipe and bring them all here, then change them back into humans and we'll take them home."

Finn shook his head. "I'm sorry. That cannot be done."

"Why?"

"My magic isn't strong enough," said Finn.

"Then let Jakob try."

Finn shook his head again. "With respect, Marianna, you do not understand the complexity of the task. Elvendale is vast. There's no telling how far some of the children have traveled. How long do we wait for them? How long would it take a snail to reach us? How would a salmon swim up a dry mountain path? And some of them . . ."

". . . might be dead," finished Marianna. "And whose fault is that?"

"Please, Mari, calm down," said Moller. "Listen. Do you hear what I'm saying? We can't go back. We can't lie for the rest of our lives."

Marianna turned to her brother. "What do you say, Jakob? You're keeping very quiet."

Jakob took a deep breath and sighed it away. "I think Papa's right," he said. "I don't want to face them, Mari. You don't know what it was like— you weren't there. But after you'd gone . . . being the only child left . . . it was awful. And it'll be the same again. Everywhere we go, there will be people staring at us, muttering and cursing, wishing we were someone else."

Marianna hung her head. She knew she was defeated.

Finn approached one of the arches. "This tunnel leads to a different part of Hamelin Hill," he said. "There is a small town nearby. It is a welcoming place—far enough away from Hamelin for you to live unrecognized, but close enough to feel familiar. I think you would do well there. Do you have a trade, Moller?"

Moller nodded. "I'm a shoemaker. But everything I own is in Hamelin. I don't have the money to set up again."

Finn smiled. "Fill your pockets with stones. And you, Jakob." He pointed to the tunnel floor.

Moller and Jakob obeyed. Finn put his pipe to his lips and started to play—just for a few seconds, but it was enough. Moller reached into his pocket and pulled out a golden coin.

"Well, look at that!" he said wonderingly. "Solid

gold! You know what this is, Jakob, don't you? This, son, is a bright future."

"Buy yourself a shop," said Finn. "You will do well, I promise. Though not, I think, in those clothes."

Moller couldn't argue with that. His clothes were muddied and torn from his travels, and Jakob and Marianna looked no better. Finn played his pipe and instantly the family was clean and newly clothed.

"So," he said, "have you decided?"

Moller looked at his children. They both seemed downcast, despite Finn's gifts, but they nodded.

"Yes, we've decided," said Moller. "Lead on."

CHAPTER
FIFTY-SEVEN

They traveled on, down a damp, low-roofed tunnel. Finn was at the front with his illuminated pipe. He was deep in thought, planning his future. Now that the curse was gone, he could return home to his family. There was nothing to stop him. Jakob had healed the stab wound as soon as they were clear of the forest, so he felt perfectly well again. He could journey south once the Mollers were safely through the hill. Should he? *Yes!* He started to tingle with excitement, just thinking about it.

Behind Finn walked Moller, then Marianna, and finally Jakob, who had insisted on being last. The reason he had given was that his staff was glowing and the light would be most useful there. But Marianna sensed there was something more.

"Jakob? What's wrong?"

There was no reply.

"I know you don't want to tell me, but I'd like to know. I might be able to help."

Marianna glanced at her brother. There was a

strange, haunted look in his eyes. Could he feel the curse, waking inside him?

"I'm fine, Mari," he said. "I feel really good. I just wonder . . . how long it will last."

Marianna felt her heart slide into her belly. It *was* the curse.

"You'll get over it," she said, trying to sound confident. "A few hours a month—that's all."

"No," said Jakob, "that's not what I meant. I'm thinking about my legs. What's going to happen to them when I leave the hill? I couldn't bear to be twisted again. Not now."

Marianna didn't know what to say. The thought had never even occurred to her. She had been so busy thinking about other problems they might face once they were home.

"It will be fine," said Marianna. "The magic will hold."

As soon as she heard the words, she wished she had kept her mouth shut. What a stupid thing to say! She couldn't promise that. She was raising Jakob's hopes. Skipping around the issue because it was too dreadful to think about. But before she could make things right, they reached the end of the tunnel.

Finn started to play his pipe and somewhere, deep in their hearts, Marianna and Jakob remembered the melody. It was the soft, sinuous one he had played to open the door from the other side.

Then the familiar blue light appeared, cutting

a door in the rock. Finn played on until the door silently swung open.

They could see the sky. A midnight blue sky, freckled with stars. Marianna moved closer. She could see a valley and a small, unfamiliar town. Everyone was sleeping but lamps were burning bright, and Marianna suddenly felt such a longing to join those people. To walk through their streets and smell their cooking. Hear their snores and their babies crying.

"It's gorgeous," she said, turning to Jakob—but he was backing away down the tunnel.

"I can't go," he said.

"What's this?" said Moller.

"I can't go, Papa," said Jakob. Tears were brimming in his eyes. "Please don't make me."

"Make you? Those days are gone, Jakob. I'll never make you do anything again, not if you don't want to. But what is this?"

Jakob was panting, frantic as a rabbit with a dog at its heels. "I don't want—I can't—not if—"

"*Sshhhh. Hush now.*" Finn's voice, soft as velvet. Jakob felt the Piper's hands on his shoulders: holding him, calming him, soothing him. The fear and worry slipped away.

Finn started to whisper in his ear. "Have no fear, Jakob. You will lose nothing. The magic will hold. But as for the curse . . . I cannot be so sure, so listen carefully now. If the Beast comes to you, do not let it be in your world. There are hunters there; you would not be safe. As the next full moon approaches, if you have *any* suspicion—if you feel *anything* different about yourself, deep inside—come back here, to this place. Strike the ground with your staff and the door will open. Come through the hill, find somewhere safe to leave your belongings. And when you feel the change coming upon you, undress and leave your clothes too.

"My hawk will fly that night. If you need me, call. I will come to you. Now go. And may good fortune go with you."

With that, Finn stepped back into the shadows. And Jakob approached the light . . . stepped through the doorway . . . and disappeared into the night beyond.

CHAPTER
FIFTY-EIGHT

"You'll never guess what just happened to me!" said Jakob, struggling in through the shop door with his arms full of bread and vegetables.

Marianna stopped sweeping and leaned on her broom. "You fought a dragon. You were in the market square, buying hot sausages, when the dragon—who was sleeping on the church roof—smelled them. And suddenly—*shoof!*—he flew down on his leathery wings, terrifying the whole town! But you fought him off with a loaf of bread."

"No," said Jakob. "Stranger than that. I thought I saw Johann, the butcher's boy."

Marianna's broom clattered to the floor.

"No!" she gasped, turning pale. "Sit down. Tell me."

"I'll put these away first," said Jakob. He slipped by her and disappeared into the family rooms behind the shop.

Marianna sat on a stool and waited for him to return. Outside, she could hear her father and a tradesman laughing out loud. The tradesman had just arrived with a smart new sign:

SIMEN MOLLER & FAMILY
~ Quality Shoemakers ~

Now he was hanging it outside the shop.

Marianna watched her father through the window. He was a changed man these days, quick to smile and determined to make a comfortable life for them all. He had found the shop on their very first day in town. It was in a perfect location—on the corner of two busy streets, next to the church—so it was strange that it was empty. It almost seemed to be waiting for them to arrive.

From the moment they had seen it, Marianna and Jakob had loved it. It had a high gable and heavy black timbers, wonderfully carved and painted with flowers. From the top rooms they could see Hamelin Hill and all the higgledy-piggledy rooftops of the town. They could each have a sunny bedroom. Moller was also delighted with the property. The shop was bright and airy, and behind it was a workshop full of shoemaker's tools. *Very* strange! All he needed was leather and cloth.

And so Moller had bought the shop with Finn's gold and the family had moved in. Three weeks had passed in a haze of hard work and happiness. The house was clean and furnished. The shelves in the shop were lined with shoes and boots. The evenings were full of stories again, sandwiched between a hearty supper and an early bed for all of them. Life was good.

There was just one dark shadow in their sunny new home. It was something no one mentioned, though they all waited for it, counting off the days, one by one.

The next full moon.

And now, here was Jakob, saying he had seen Johann, the butcher's boy. What could that mean? Was it a sign?

Jakob reappeared from the kitchen, wiping his hands on a cloth.

"So?" said Marianna. "Tell me."

"I was coming from the bakehouse," said Jakob. "I saw a lad ahead of me—quite tall, with a side of bacon slung over his shoulder—and he turned and—*oh!* For a minute, I really thought it was Johann—especially with him carrying bacon."

"But it definitely wasn't him?"

"No. How could it be?"

Marianna shook her head. Of course it couldn't be Johann. He was a salmon, swimming through the rivers of Elvendale.

"Are you all right, Mari? You look a bit . . . lost."

Marianna sighed thoughtfully. Jakob was right. She had been lost for the moment. She had been

266

back in Elvendale, by the Standing Stone, with the Piper playing and the children shape-shifting around her.

"Do you think of them sometimes?" she said. "The others?"

Jakob shrugged. "A bit. But I wasn't like you, Mari. I didn't have many friends in Hamelin. Well, I did, but they were much older. Do you remember Lemken? The old man who used to sit by the abbey? I miss him. But I don't really miss any of the children. I'm glad some of them are gone! Do you remember stinky Albert, the tanner's apprentice? He was *horrible* to me. I hope Finn turned him into something really nasty, like a cock-roach. No—a worm! Then one of the hedgehogs could eat him."

"That's a terrible thing to say!" exclaimed Marianna, but she couldn't hide her smile. "You're right, though. It was different for me. I used to gossip with my friends and share secrets. I miss that. And the worst thing is, I don't know what happened to them. We were all changing at the same time and there were so many of us, I don't know who became what. And I *still* don't understand why the Piper did it."

"He wasn't thinking," said Jakob. "He did it because he could: that's what he told me. Elves are like that sometimes. And I know you think it was a terrible thing to do, Mari, but some of them will be living good lives. Can you imagine how brilliant it must be for the ones that became birds? No work, just endless flying! I would love that."

"So would I—for a while. But for the rest of my life? I don't think so. And you're forgetting Karl. His life is over."

Jakob shrugged again. "That was the Beast, not Finn."

Marianna said nothing, simply looked at her brother. Was this a good time to talk about the curse? Surely he must be desperately worried. The full moon was just three days away.

But Jakob seemed to read her mind and, before she could say anything, he had escaped out of the door. Through the window, she could see him with Moller, admiring the newly hung sign as if he didn't have a worry in the world.

Marianna shook her head wonderingly and returned to her broom.

"I've finished here," she said, looking at the clean floor. "Upstairs next. And worry about something else, Marianna!"

As she started to climb the stairs, she thought about supper. Up to the first floor . . . to the second . . . to the third she went. By the time she reached Jakob's room, her head was full of meat and vegetables. But when she saw what was in his room, she forgot supper in an instant.

In the corner of the room, propped up against the wall, was Jakob's wooden staff.

It was kept well polished, but it wasn't being used. Jakob hadn't done any magic since Elvendale and he didn't need it for support. His body had remained strong and firm and supple, just as the Piper had promised. So the staff was simply lying there in the shadows, dark and dormant.

Only it wasn't dark any longer.

It was glowing.

CHAPTER
FIFTY-NINE

The staff was glowing with a dull red light, like blood in water. Marianna fetched Jakob from the street. Dragged him upstairs. Pulled him into the room and pointed. Jakob said nothing, simply stared. The staff hadn't been like that an hour earlier when he was last in the room.

Jakob didn't know what to think. He felt perfectly well. No fever or tiredness. No sense of a shadow moving within him, as Finn had described. But the staff wouldn't glow for no reason at all. He knew that. It was a warning. It was telling him to prepare. Telling him to return to Elvendale.

Marianna wanted Jakob to leave right away. She was terrified he would transform there and then, and they wouldn't be able to restrain him. He would smash his way out of the house and rampage through the town. The townsfolk would scream in terror and call for a hunter. His poor dead body would be dragged through the streets and burned on a bonfire. She could see it all so clearly.

But Jakob wanted to wait. He said he would leave on the day itself, and he did. Marianna and his father went with him. They climbed up Hamelin Hill, back to the place they had all committed to memory in case this desperate moment came.

Jakob struck his staff against the ground and waited. Soon the blue light appeared.

"Let me come with you," begged Marianna. The outline of a door was visible in the hillside.

Jakob shook his head.

"I don't suppose you want me either, do you?" said Moller, his voice sounding strangely hoarse.

Jakob smiled and shook his head again.

"Off you go, then," said Moller. "We'll be thinking of you."

Jakob nodded, not trusting himself to speak. He swallowed hard and walked through the open door. And then, just before it closed, he turned and raised his staff high in the air.

Moller and Marianna saw him silhouetted against the dazzling blue light.

"Hurrah for Sir Jakob of the New Legs!" he cried. "Off on a new quest!"

Then the door closed. He was gone.

CHAPTER
SIXTY

Jakob walked through Hamelin Hill, making a mental note of all the twists and turns in the tunnels. He wanted to able to find his way back when it was over. He reached Elvendale late in the afternoon, walked down the hillside into the vale and looked for a suitable place to change. He soon found it: a small stand of trees, away from the road, with a sizable pool and a low flat stone that could serve as a bench.

He sat down on the stone and waited for night to fall.

It was a long wait, broken only by a fluttering of fire-gold wings as a hawk swept in and landed on a low bough.

It shook itself, straightened a ruffled feather, and stared at Jakob with its dark eyes. But it remained silent and Jakob had just about decided it wasn't Flyte when the bird spoke.

"Finn is close by, should you need him. Luck be with you." With that, Flyte disappeared into the darkening sky.

Jakob smiled. The news was reassuring, though he hoped he would cope on his own. He certainly didn't want anyone watching him when he changed. That would be too embarrassing.

Night came. The moon rose and began its long, slow journey across the sky. Jakob looked at his hands. He wasn't sprouting hairs. His teeth didn't seem to be growing, and there was no smell. Marianna had told him about the Beast's foul stench. There was no sign of that, thank the Lord, but there was still time.

An hour went by. Two. The midnight moon was high now, nearing the zenith. Jakob could feel his heart thumping in his chest. He was starting to feel sick. "It's fear," he told himself. "Not the curse." But he couldn't be sure.

The moon slipped into its highest position. Jakob saw it happen. Actually saw it jolt into place, like a bolt on a wagon. Then he felt it begin. A moving— a quickening—deep inside him.

He stood up and pulled off his clothes, fingers fumbling with the laces. He was shaking all over and couldn't stop it. He closed his eyes and hoped the sensation would go away, but it didn't. He felt ripples moving up and down his body, as if the curse was exploring him, deciding what to do with its new host.

Jakob looked at his hands.

"Oh, dear Lord."

There were long silver hairs shooting out of the skin. Not just on his hands—on his arms and chest. On his belly, legs, and back. Then he felt a warm, tingling sensation in his toes and, as he watched in horror, his feet changed shape. His legs stretched and remolded themselves, till they became so long and spindly at the bottom, he couldn't stand upright anymore. He was thrown forward onto all fours.

He started to quiver. The tingling was happening all over his body now, but there was no pain. No pain at all. No breaking bones, no stretching flesh, no straining muscles, no falling into darkness. No sense of the Beast taking him over, body, brain, and soul. Just the warm, caressive tingling and an unexpected feeling that something truly wondrous was happening.

And then the tingling stopped. It was done. He had changed.

Jakob stood quite still for a moment, wondering what to do next. His eyes were drawn to the pool. Could he see himself? See what he had become?

He walked forward, surprised at how natural it felt to move on all fours. Marianna had said the same when she described being a fox. He hadn't believed her at the time but now he knew it was true.

Jakob reached the pool and looked down into the water. He saw the moon, rich and round like a great silver platter—and he saw a wolf. Not a Beast.

A wolf. A glorious silver gray wolf, with amber eyes and a black-lipped muzzle. He was extraordinarily handsome. The most magical creature he had ever seen.

Then he heard something. A tiny sound—a twig snapping—but his ears caught it and he whipped around, fangs bared.

It was the Piper.

Finn stared at Jakob, completely overwhelmed by what he was seeing. "You are *magnificent*," he said at last. "Just *wondrous*. I feared for you, Jakob. The Beast was so strong and you are so young. But this . . . This is not the Beast. This is not a curse. This is a gift. The Spirit of the Forest has given you the gift of belonging, Jakob. You are a prince of the forest. A king of the night. Enjoy your gift, Jakob. Use it! Run, my friend. Run as you have never run before!"

And Jakob did run, all through the night and on till dawn, while the moon spread her silver cloak over the land before him. Rivers and fields, forests and farms—all passed by in a flying tapestry of shade and shadow. And there was no hunting or killing for Jakob. When he awoke the next morning, there was no blood on his tongue. No fur tagged in his teeth. No dark, shameful secrets to hide.

There was sunshine and birdsong. A tiredness in his limbs from running all night. A boyish longing for breakfast. And in his heart, there was such a tumble of emotion. So much joy! Had ever a boy been given such a gift? To run as a wolf, with the wind at his heels, through a glorious night of wild magic?

There was wonder and exhilaration. A burning desire to do it all again! But there was something else too. *Relief.* Sheer, blessed relief that it was over. He had survived. Now he could go home.

CHAPTER
SIXTY-ONE

It was well past midday when Jakob reached the town. He walked through the streets and couldn't help noticing that everyone was friendly. Every smile he gave was returned, often with a nod and a greeting. One kind woman handed him a bread roll.

"You look as hungry as a wolf!" she declared. "Aren't they feeding you at home?"

Jakob grinned, thanked her, and walked on, munching happily. Through the market square he went, around the corner and on to his own street. And then a curious thing happened. As soon as he saw his father's shop, his heart gave a bump and he felt a warm, happy feeling deep inside. He quickened his pace, suddenly longing to be there.

But when he reached the shop, he didn't go inside. Instead, he looked through the window.

Marianna was behind the counter, tying ribbons onto a pair of red satin shoes. She was wearing her elf-berry necklace! The one he had given her! That was unusual. She kept it in a box in her bedroom and

277

said it was too precious to wear. But today she had put it on: her little piece of Elvendale. Did she hope it would bring him luck? Keep him safe? Perhaps. Jakob smiled. It was lovely to have a sister who cared.

Then his father came out of the workshop. Like Marianna, he looked desperately worried. He had dark circles under his eyes, as if he hadn't slept, and his hands were restless. He said something to Marianna, then stroked her hair and gently kissed her cheek. In return, Marianna gave him a smile, but it was small and fleeting. And Jakob suddenly realized: they didn't know he was safe and well. To them, he was still missing. He could be lost. Injured. Trapped inside the Beast's body. Lying dead on a hillside.

Jakob smiled. When they saw him, they would be so happy. And that was how his life was going to be from now on. *Happy*. Quiet, cheerful, and loving, with food on the table, a warm comfortable bed, and the sweetest of dreams. And then, every full moon, there would be excitement and adventure. Meetings with Finn, lessons in magic, and wild, exhilarating runs beneath the stars. The whole of Elvendale was his to explore, from the Kerin Hills in the north to the Morvern Mountains in the south.

That wasn't a bad life for a poor boy from Hamelin, was it?

Jakob grinned: a heartfelt, dazzling beam of happiness that lit up his face and tickled his ears. He smoothed down his hair, lifted the door latch, and stepped inside.

278

Acknowledgments

As ever, love and thanks to:

Everyone at Puffin UK, especially Yvonne Hooker and Wendy Tse.

Academi, for the award of a writer's grant to fund my research trip to Hamelin in May 2006.

Pat White at Rogers, Coleridge and White.

Rob Soldat, for his help, support, and convivial company on long car journeys.

And, finally, endless love and thanks to Ray, for doing the best he can.